Dear Romance Reader,

Welcome to a world of breathtaking passion and never-ending romance.

Welcome to ***Precious Gem Romances.***

It is our pleasure to present *Precious Gem Romances,* a wonderful new line of romance books by some of America's best-loved authors. Let these thrilling historical and contemporary romances sweep you away to far-off times and places in stories that will dazzle your senses and melt your heart.

Sparkling with joy, laughter, and love, each *Precious Gem Romance* glows with all the passion and excitement you expect from the very best in romance. Offered at a great affordable price, these books are an irresistible value—and an essential addition to your romance collection. Tender love stories you will want to read again and again, *Precious Gem Romances* are books you will treasure forever.

Look for fabulous new *Precious Gem Romances* each month—available only at Wal★Mart.

Lynn Brown, Publisher

LOUISIANA BRIDE

SHAUNA MICHAELS

ZEBRA BOOKS
Kensington Publishing Corp.
http://www.zebrabooks.com

To my mother, Catherine, and my mother-in-law, Marcella. Both great ladies have been a wonderful inspiration to me.

ZEBRA BOOKS are published by

Kensington Publishing Corp.
850 Third Avenue
New York, NY 10022

Copyright © 1999 by Margaret Daley

All rights reserved. No part of this book may be reproduced in any form or by any means without the prior written consent of the Publisher, excepting brief quotes used in reviews.

If you purchased this book without a cover you should be aware that this book is stolen property. It was reported as "unsold and destroyed" to the Publisher and neither the Author nor the Publisher has received any payment for this "stripped book."

Zebra and the Z logo Reg. U.S. Pat. & TM Off.

First Printing: March, 1999
10 9 8 7 5 4 3 2 1

Printed in the United States of America

ONE

Fall, 1720

Racing along the stone path, Danielle de Bussy escaped into the garden before the Marquis saw her. She dragged in deep breaths to calm her pounding heart and sank down onto the bench to wait, arranging her *contouche* of pink taffeta so she would look perfect for Pierre. She had taken a long time to get ready for him, choosing her favorite, a gown with matching pink ribbons that fastened the dress down the front.

She looked about in anticipation. Pierre would be here any minute. Had he changed? Did he still love her? Would he ask the Marquis for her hand in marriage today? Impatient, she peered around the hedge that concealed her from the chateau. Where *was* Pierre?

The chilling breeze swept multicolored leaves along the path. Trembling, Danielle pulled her wool shawl about her and tapped her foot, trying to ignore the coldness seeping into her. She would do anything for him. He and Sister Mary Catherine were the only two people who cared what happened to her.

When she and Pierre married, she would leave Chateau Duchamp and never see the Marquis again.

He would no longer control her life once she was the wife of the future Comte DuBois.

For the past two years, only her visits to the abbey and the letters from Pierre had kept her going. Now he was home and everything would be all right. She smiled, feeling hope for the first time in a long while.

"Ah, I remember that smile. I've carried it here for two years." Pierre touched his chest.

Danielle leaped to her feet and threw her arms around him, raining kisses all over his face. Her shawl slipped to the stone bench, the coldness forgotten as she nestled into his embrace. "I was beginning to fear that I'd dreamed your letter or that Margot had forged it as some cruel joke."

"Papa had some last-minute business at the estate. I had to wait until he was through."

"Have you told your father?"

Pierre laughed. "Always direct. I had forgotten that."

Danielle leaned back and stared up into his handsome face, every line carved into her memory. "Have you?"

His hazel eyes became serious, a frown marring the perfection of his features. "No, I haven't had a chance. I arrived only last night. This invitation from the Marquis took me by surprise." He avoided her gaze.

A shiver flashed up her spine. Danielle finally noticed the cold. "Come, sit and tell me about court life." Scooping up her shawl and wrapping it about her shoulders, she sat on the bench. "I can't wait until I can go. I've heard such stories about Versailles. I want to know everything—what the women wear, what the men wear, what Louis—"

Still standing, Pierre laid his finger over her mouth. "Shh, we'll have time later for those stories. The Marquis expects us in the library. I offered to find you when the servants couldn't."

Whenever her stepfather wanted to punish her for some imagined misdeed, he called her to his library. The cold lanced deeper into her. "Hold me, Pierre."

That was the closest Danielle would come to saying she was scared. She had lived under the Marquis's reign of terror for ten of her eighteen years. She didn't trust anything he did. When her mother had married the Marquis, she had cherished hopes that he would be like her father—kind, charming—and at first he had been. Quickly, however, everything had changed as she and her mother discovered the true nature of the man. Another shiver pierced her heart, as though she sensed her life was about to change.

Pierre's arms around her were comforting. When he lifted her chin and touched his lips to hers, she blocked the fear from her mind for a brief moment. Of course her life was about to change. Pierre was home. Soon she would be free of the Marquis. She drew solace from that fact until she and Pierre began walking toward the chateau. Her fear returned with each step she took toward the massive structure. Such evil lay behind its beautiful facade.

Pierre was here. Nothing could happen to her as long as he was beside her. She repeated that reassurance over and over in her mind as she neared the library, wishing she could flee. Soon. When they were married, she would be rid of the Marquis.

When she heard her stepfather's hearty laugh followed by Margot's giggle, Danielle stopped, her eyes round, her hands clammy. Though they were inside, she still felt chilled to the bone, the acid taste of fear in her mouth.

"Danielle?" Pierre reached for her hand. He caressed her pale cheeks, his eyes tenderly conveying his support. "I'd never let anyone hurt you. I love you. Remember that."

Those words were all she needed to brave the next few minutes. "I know. I love you, Pierre." She traced the outline of the mouth that had so gently possessed hers only moments before, his full lips soft beneath her touch.

"Danielle!" The sharp whip of her stepfather's voice cut her.

Stiffening, she dropped her hands to her sides as Pierre stepped away. She wouldn't cower before the Marquis's look of condemnation. Instead, she walked past her stepfather into the library as if she had nothing in the world to be afraid of.

As she advanced into the center of the room, she scanned the faces of the people present. Colette, her mother, was seated in a brocade chair, her look impassive, almost vacant. There would be no help from her. Danielle had learned years ago that her mother could not stand up to the Marquis to protect her only child; she wasn't strong enough to withstand her husband's cruelty. Danielle had given up turning to her mother for help, placing a guilty burden on her. Since her mother's remarriage, Danielle had relied only on herself.

When Danielle's gaze rested on Margot, it narrowed. With her squared neckline and a corset that tried to slim her generous waistline, thus pushing up her breasts and exposing her overflowing cleavage, Margot looked as though she were several years Danielle's senior, rather than six months younger. Margot smiled before flipping open her silk-embroidered fan to hide her smug expression.

When Danielle had first come to Chateau Duchamp, she had been excited about having a sister. She had wanted brothers and sisters and had hated being left to find her own companionship. But after thirty minutes alone with Margot, all her enthusiasm had died under her stepsister's taunting tongue. Even though she had continued to try to be Margot's friend, she soon had realized that her stepsister cared only for herself and wanted no competition for her father's affections.

Danielle didn't take the chair between her mother and Margot but stood between Comte DuBois and Pierre and faced her family. The Marquis handed everyone a glass of red Bordeaux. Pierre wouldn't let anything happen, she thought, and managed to tamp down her apprehension.

His triumphant look fixed on her, the Marquis raised his goblet. "I want to offer a toast to the marriage contract between our neighbor, Pierre DuBois and"—the Marquis paused, a gleam brightening his eyes—"and my daughter, Margot. May they have many years of happiness together."

Danielle felt the color drain from her face. Her glass slid from her numbed fingers and shattered on the carpet at her feet. "No, it is not true!" The words, wrenched from her parched throat, echoed in the suddenly silent room. Everyone stared at her.

Shock held her immobile as the pool of wine spread at her feet, staining her pink gown. The faces of her family blurred, and she fought desperately for control. She squeezed her eyes closed, her breath trapped in her lungs. In her mind's eye she saw Margot's malicious sneer, the fleur-de-lis beauty mark painted next to her stepsister's lips taunting her.

Opening her eyes, she looked straight at the Marquis. Before her courage failed her, she said, "I am the eldest. It is customary I should marry first."

A smirk curled the Marquis's lips. "True. Perhaps I will arrange a marriage for you." He paused again, heightening the tension in the room with his menacing silence. "But not to Pierre. The contract has been signed."

The finality in his voice imparted the hopelessness of the situation more than his words. Unless Comte DuBois broke off the marriage, Margot and Pierre would wed. Danielle refused to think about whom the Marquis might choose for her. She turned to Pierre, silently pleading for his help. He stared straight ahead and wouldn't meet her eyes.

"Pierre? Please do something!" Danielle no longer cared that everyone was witness to her appeal.

When his gaze finally embraced hers, it was full of despair, his face ashen, his mouth slashed in a grim line. She knew she would get no help from Pierre because, like her, his father controlled his life.

Danielle shifted her attention to her mother, wishing that for once she would stand up to the Marquis. But when she stared down at the folded hands in her mother's lap, Danielle knew, as always, she would say nothing.

The Marquis continued as though nothing had transpired. "This is a momentous day for our families, uniting the two adjoining estates in marriage. We won't wait too long for the wedding. I know how eager these two young people are—"

The oppressive air closed in on Danielle. Her chest hurt from trying to drag in a breath. She couldn't stay another second in the room. Outside in the hall, she doubled over, her teeth digging into her lower lip to stifle her cry. The taste of her own blood was as bitter as her situation. She welcomed the pain that spread through her, hoping it might block the anguish she felt in her heart. It didn't.

Laughter from the library filled her mind and propelled her up the stairs to her bedchamber. She couldn't listen to their happiness when she was dying inside. Pierre had been her future, her hope, her escape.

With angry strides, she paced from the fireplace—where a warm fire gave the room a soft glow—to her canopied bed, trying to figure out how she could stop the marriage. She would implore Pierre to run away to Paris. She had always wanted to see Versailles. Comte DuBois loved Pierre; he would forgive him in time.

Danielle didn't know Margot was in the room until her stepsister said, "*Papa* sent me to see if you were ill."

Danielle whirled around. "Get out!"

Clicking her tongue, Margot shook her head. "This is the way you greet your dear sister? I wanted you to help plan my wedding. I know you ache to be part of it."

She closed the door and moved farther into the chamber. A cold, satisfied smile dimpled her full cheeks, distorting the fake beauty mark. "Pierre's such a dear. I can't wait until our wedding night. Maybe I won't wait now that we are pledged to each other. I've seen how he looks at me. It should be a very fulfilling union."

Danielle's fingernails cut into the palms of her hands. "And let him know you aren't a virgin? He could use that as grounds to nullify the contract. Not very clever of you."

Margot flew at Danielle, burying her fingers in Danielle's blonde curls. Danielle fell to the floor, pinned beneath Margot, who still yanked at Danielle's hair.

With a strength Danielle hadn't thought possible, she shoved Margot off, then rolled on top of her stepsister, securing her flailing arms to the floor. Danielle wanted to tear off Margot's powdered wig to expose her mousy brown hair, to wipe away the overdone makeup that covered pox scars. She wanted to expose Margot's physical ugliness as well as her cruelty.

Steely talons dug into Danielle's shoulders, jerking her to her feet. The Marquis spun her about. His mouth contorted into an angry, slashing line before he slapped her face and sent her staggering back several feet. Pain shot through her jaw; her mind reeled from the force.

The Marquis lifted Margot off the floor. *"L'enfant,* did she hurt you?"

"Yes, *Papa."* Tears cascaded down Margot's

chubby cheeks, marring the white powder and red rouge she wore. "I came up here to see if she was all right and she attacked me."

"I did not!" Danielle shouted, knowing even as she protested that it was useless. Margot was always right in her father's eyes.

"Leave us. I'll take care of Danielle."

"Can't I stay, *Papa?*" Margot stopped all pretense of crying.

"Another time. Pierre and his father await your return."

Reluctantly, Margot left the bedchamber. The click of the door reverberated throughout the room, echoing Danielle's fate. They faced each other in silence. The tension stretched her nerves to their limit, as he intended. Part of his pleasure had always been in using a person's imagination to his advantage. She would not allow him to win this battle of wills.

"I've been patient with you until now." The Marquis's whisper was edged with malice. "But I cannot tolerate your hurting my precious. I must teach you obedience. Your future husband will thank me—if I arrange a marriage for you." His lewd gaze flared as it traveled over her body. "Like a wild horse, you need to be broken."

There was no doubt in her mind what the Marquis meant. As he advanced toward her, she moved backward until her legs hit the side of her bed, alarming her.

His tongue slithered over his lips as he blocked her escape. He ran his soft hand over the red welt on her cheek, admiring his work. "There are other places where I could slap you."

She struggled to break free, but his hand gripped

the back of her neck and he thrust his body against hers. She nearly retched when his bulging manhood pressed against her stomach. "You won't get away with this. I'll scream until Pierre comes up here."

His eyes were hard and penetrating as he thought over her words. "Yes, you would."

Smiling coldly, he shoved her down onto the bed and clamped his hand over her mouth before she had time to react. His sneer broadened as he trapped her against the mattress. His free hand glided downward, lifting the skirt of her gown until he found the soft flesh of her inner thigh.

Her stomach knotted as sour bile rose in her throat. His blunt fingers crept upward, and she writhed frenetically beneath his pawing. She would fight him until she didn't have a breath left in her.

As quickly as he began, he stopped and pulled back. "But I would rather savor the sweet moment to come in my mind, as I know you will." His leer touched each of her intimate places. "I'll return after our guests depart. No one will help you in this house. I'll relish your screams then."

The click of the lock struck her as forcibly as the Marquis's slap. Danielle pushed herself to a sitting position. *This is happening to someone else. It can't be happening to me.* But as she silently denied it, the knowledge she would be raped by the night's end assailed her. Frantic, she looked about her for an escape. She couldn't sit and wait for him to ravage her. She had never been able to wait for her fate.

As though possessed by a demon, Danielle rushed to the door and tried the handle. When the door wouldn't open—as she had guessed it wouldn't—she pounded her fists into the wood, imagining it to be the face of the Marquis. Again and again she screamed, "Let me out," praying that somehow Pierre would hear her and come to her rescue.

But no one came. Her hands bloodied and throbbing with pain, she collapsed to the floor, no longer able to lift her arms. She wanted to cry, but tears wouldn't save her. Instead, she searched her room for a weapon. Her gaze fell upon the candelabrum, and she scrambled to her feet to get it.

Footsteps sounded in the hall. Quickly, with a calmness that surprised her, Danielle removed the unlit candles. With the candelabrum in her hand, she positioned herself behind the door as it was unlocked. She raised her arm.

The door was half open when her mother said, "Danielle?"

She dropped the candelabrum and pulled her mother into the room, closing the door behind her. "What are you doing here, *Maman?* Where's the Marquis?"

"In the library drinking some brandy before—" Her mother's eyelashes swept down to conceal her sadness.

"Before he rapes me."

Her mother nodded and looked up into Danielle's face, a new determination in her countenance. "But he won't if I can help it. I wanted to be a better mother to you. I thought I was doing the right thing when I married the Marquis. He was such a powerful, wealthy man. I knew we would be taken care of. I didn't realize the kind of man he was. I won't let him ruin your chance at happiness."

"But he has. He has taken from me the man I love."

"You can't fight the Marquis. I tried when we were first married."

The pain that flashed into her mother's eyes wrenched Danielle. She felt hopeless and helpless. *"Maman—"*

Her mother shook her head. "Listen to me, Danielle. I want you to go to the abbey. Seek protection from the sisters. Your Uncle Robert lives in the Louisiana Colony. Perhaps Sister Mary Catherine can find a way to send you there. That's your only hope. The Marquis is too powerful in France for you to stay."

"Come with me. If he discovers you helped me, he'll beat you."

"I can't. He'll come after us both. No one defies him, especially his wife."

"But I can't—"

"No, Danielle. I have stood by and watched him belittle you for years. He won't have what should be your husband's right." Swiftly her mother hugged her, kissing her on both cheeks. "You must go, now, before he comes. I will always be with you here." Her mother placed her hand over Danielle's heart.

After retrieving her velvet cloak from the wardrobe, Danielle embraced her mother once more, afraid this might be the last time she saw her. "I love you."

"And I you. Now go!"

Swallowing the tears that clogged her throat, Danielle eased the door open, relieved to find the hallway empty. Scurrying down the corridor, she paused at the top of the staircase to glance back at her mother. A tear slipped down her cheeks at the sight of her mother alone by the bedchamber door.

"Maman," Danielle whispered and took a step back toward her mother, wanting to beg her to come to the abbey.

Her mother motioned to her to leave. Danielle's heart throbbed slowly against her breast at the thought of never seeing her mother after this evening. Again Colette waved her arm, dismissing her daughter. A lump formed in Danielle's throat, her tears blurring her vision.

"Somehow I will find a way to rescue you, *Maman,"* she whispered to herself as she raced toward the front door.

"Going somewhere, my pet?"

She faltered for a second at the sound of the Marquis's voice, but resumed her flight. Ten feet to freedom. Five. His fingers clawed into her waist as though he were an animal capturing his prey. He dragged her back against his solid frame.

"Now that I've decided to have you, you won't escape. Bridget has begun to bore me."

The mention of the Marquis's mistress, who lived under the same roof as her mother, enraged Danielle. It was another humiliation her mother had suffered at the hands of the Marquis. Desperate and frantic, she struggled within the tight band of her stepfather's arms. Years of hatred gave her strength she hadn't realized she possessed as she thrashed and kicked. Her foot connected with his shin.

The Marquis yelled, his arms loosening about her. Seizing the moment, she twisted free and ran for the door. Her hand was on the knob when he gripped her free hand and yanked her toward him. She clung to the knob, determined not to let go.

But her strength was waning, and his fingers bit into her flesh.

She wouldn't last another minute in this tug-of-war; she had to think of something. Suddenly she went slack, letting go of the knob. The Marquis stumbled back. As he steadied himself, his hands still locked about her wrist, she lunged for the candelabrum always kept on a table near the front door. Without a second's hesitation, she lifted the cold silver and brought it down upon his head. His eyes widened; his body slumped against her as he sank to the marble floor.

Her breaths rapid, she stepped over his large frame and thrust the front door open. Outside, the fall air cooled her heated body, but she didn't pause to relish its freshness. She fled the chateau, refusing to think about what she had just done.

She considered taking a horse from the stable, but there were always guards posted because of the Marquis's prize stallions. She would have to cross the fields and get to Pierre before the Marquis awakened. Pierre would know what to do. Pierre would protect her.

When she reached Chateau DuBois, Danielle guessed it to be just after midnight. She stood before the imposing structure, its three-story facade bathed in soft moonlight, trying to decide how to let Pierre know she was there. She concluded she'd best march up to the front door and ask to see him.

The manservant on duty was an old, familiar retainer. Jacques hid his surprise at seeing her there at such an unusual hour. She immediately asked for Pierre. While the old retainer shuffled toward the stairs, Danielle began to pace, nervous, not sure how to explain to Pierre what had happened at Chateau Duchamp. She clung to the fact that Pierre loved her, not Margot.

A few minutes later, Pierre hurried down the stairs, confused and concerned. He pulled her into the grand salon. "Why are you here?"

She laughed, partly from nerves and partly because she was so relieved to be safe. Instead of answering Pierre, she wound her arms around him, savoring the shelter of his protection. For a few seconds he remained rigid. Then, slowly, his arms twined about her.

"I never want to leave."

"But, Danielle, you can't stay here."

She leaned away from Pierre to stare up into his face. "I must. The Marquis tried to rape me tonight."

Pierre's jaw twitched in anger. "Perhaps you misunderstood."

Danielle backed away. "Misunderstood! I know what goes on between a man and a woman. Bridget took pleasure in telling me every detail." She recalled vividly everything Bridget had told her about satisfying a man. It was something Danielle had been prepared to do for Pierre because it was known that men craved the pleasure, but she knew she wouldn't enjoy submitting to it. What the Marquis had tried to do tonight had only confirmed her feelings about the act.

"Danielle, I can do nothing."

"We can run away to Paris—marry, as we had planned. Your father will forgive you in time."

His shoulders sagged; a frown lined his face. "It's impossible."

For the first time, Danielle noticed the increasing distance Pierre put between them, the agony in his expression. She had to acknowledge the hopelessness that laced his words. "Why?"

"I must marry Margot."

She tensed. "You desire it?"

"No. No!"

Relaxing her taut shoulders, she smiled. "Marriage contracts have been broken before."

"If only it were that simple, Danielle." Pierre looked away. "The Marquis would ruin my father. He holds my father's markers."

"But you're the only hope I have!" Panic flooded her like a river swollen by spring rains.

He crossed the room and embraced her. "I'm sorry. Please forgive me. I have no choice."

"But if he finds me—"

"You must go to the abbey. I'll take you. The sisters will protect you." Pierre grabbed her hand and was already pulling her toward the grand salon's door.

Numb, Danielle no longer cared what happened to her. She allowed Pierre to draw her toward the stable. They couldn't marry, so it made no difference where she went—as long as it wasn't back to Chateau Duchamp.

Winter, 1720

Rouen Beauvoir tore up the letter from his father, tossing the pieces into the fire. Anger carved deep into his tanned features as he leaned against the mantel and stared into the blaze. *Mon Dieu!* Couldn't his father leave him alone? He had performed his duty to the family for three long, miserable years.

Rouen had thought by coming thousands of miles to the Louisiana Colony he could forget those years of trying to prove himself to a man who neither cared nor knew how to love anyone except Henri. Rouen's eyes darkened; his throat closed. His older brother Henri and his son were dead, killed in an accident. Now his father wanted Rouen to return to France.

It is your duty as the next Duc de Beauvoir to come home, marry again, and produce heirs. His father's words filled Rouen's mind. *By the time you return home, Liliane will be free to marry again.*

Rouen struck the mantel with his fist. The pain spread up his arm. Liliane had loved him, not Henri, but she had betrothed herself to his brother. He had been forced to watch the woman he loved marry another, been forced to endure having the woman he loved bear his brother's child.

His father had arranged Rouen's marriage to Antoinette, a fragile girl who had died miscarrying. Poor Antoinette. After they had wed, she confessed she had wanted to become a nun, but her father hadn't permitted it. He wanted Antoinette to marry and strengthen his political ties at court. Why couldn't people control their own destiny?

One day he would have to give this all up, but he would set the terms. Never again would he allow another to control him. Never again would he give his heart to another; the pain of losing a loved one was too much to bear. He wouldn't marry Liliane because his father commanded it. Though he had begged her to run away with him, she chose to stay in France and marry his brother. He had been willing to defy his father; she hadn't.

He would return to France when he was ready. He had carved out a home for himself in the wilderness, foot by grueling foot. The hard work required in the New World had contrasted with the frivolous existence he had lived at Chateau Beauvoir and especially at Versailles. The primitiveness of this land lured him, appealing to a savage need to forget that other life, to forget that he had once loved and been forsaken.

"Rouen?"

He blinked, focusing on the present at Riverview. Masking the pain he felt at his brother's death, he asked the man entering the room, "Is everything ready?"

"Yes," Claude replied. "We can ride out at dawn."

"Good." Rouen stared back down at the dying fire, dismissing his friend and returning to his own private thoughts.

But Claude didn't leave. "Have you forgotten your engagement with Governor Bienville?"

Rouen shook his head.

"I'll bring Dancer 'round for you," Claude said to Rouen's back.

When the door to his office closed, Rouen relaxed. He had to finish his report; he needed to warn the Minister of Finance about the restlessness of the Chickasaw Indians. When he returned from his hunting trip with Claude, he hoped to have more proof to offer the Minister of Finance. All he had now were rumors. The Spanish had already tried to wrest the Louisiana Colony from the French. It was only a matter of time before the English openly tried also.

After finishing his report, he left his office and quickly strode outside. He felt confined, restless, and he welcomed the fresh, cold air. But even the chill in the air couldn't quiet his guilt. He had loved his older brother, but their last years together had been spent with a wedge between them, put there by their father and Liliane. Now Rouen would have no opportunity to tell Henri that he understood why his older brother had married Liliane. Duty had been bred into them from an early age by their father. Rouen wished he could tell Henri that he forgave him.

The winter cold, carried on a north wind, sliced through Rouen on the ride to Fort Louis. He scanned the flat terrain of the pine forest. Thoughts of returning to France continued to torment him. He was sure on this new ship that had laid anchor off the coastal island there was another letter from his father demanding his return. Since that letter telling of his brother's death, he hadn't replied to his father. He couldn't postpone it much longer; the Duc wasn't a patient man.

When Rouen entered Bienville's headquarters at the fort, he was surprised to find Monsieur Delon in the hallway. They greeted each other as if they were mere acquaintances, not comrades in secrecy.

As Delon passed Rouen to leave, he whispered, "Meet me at dusk by the stream on the road to your plantation."

Rouen nodded once as the door to Bienville's office opened and Monsieurs David and Pinart came into the hallway, followed by the governor.

"Ah, Rouen, I had almost given up on you. We were just leaving for the quay," Bienville announced.

On the walk to the jetty, Monsieurs David and Pinart hung back from the group, talking in low tones. Rouen glanced back at the pair and asked, "What has brought Monsieur David here?"

"He arranges a shipment of furniture. I think he also comes to examine the cargo on the *La Baleine*—as do many of the men in the colony. These *casquette* girls are the future for us. We are in Sister Gertrude's debt for bringing yet another cargo of marriageable women here."

"True," Rouen said. "They aren't lightskirts, but girls raised in a nunnery."

"Exactly my point. Families are what carve homes out of this wilderness. Thankfully some people in France understand we need women who will make a good home for a man and give him children."

"Why is Pinart meeting *La Baleine?*" Rouen didn't care for the suggestion in the governor's voice. "Isn't he satisfied having already killed one wife? Must he seek another?"

Bienville scowled. "I have no proof Pinart murdered his wife. She fell."

"With more bruises and injuries than that fall should have caused."

"Don't cause trouble, Rouen. I know you can take care of yourself, but Pinart is an expert swordsman. If anything were to happen to you, your father would have my skin inch by inch. I don't care to come up against Beauvoir at court. I have enough trouble getting what I need for this colony."

Rouen clamped his jaws down. His father hadn't cared what he did with his life until Henri and Paul's deaths. Rouen felt his father's prison reaching him even here.

Booted feet sounded on the cypress planks as the group of men made their way to the end of the jetty, where the smell of saltwater and rotting fish hung in the cold air. Twelve young women and one nun huddled together in the small craft. The two crewmen from *La Baleine* rowed to the pier and tied up, then helped the women climb from the longboat.

Rouen impassively studied each woman's face as she left the swaying craft. Their expressions were filled with fear and exhaustion. Bienville claimed these *casquettes* would be the colony's future. Right now they looked ready to flee back to the ship if given the chance.

His thoughts began to wander as the women lined up behind the nun talking with Bienville. Rouen was already thinking about his meeting with Delon later that afternoon when the last woman to leave the boat caught his attention. It wasn't her height, even though she was several inches taller than the other women. It wasn't her waist-length blonde hair that danced in the wet, cold breeze—hair only partially covered by a mobcap. It was the look on her face that arrested Rouen. There was a challenge in her dark eyes, as if she intended to take on the world and win. He was intrigued.

Rouen stepped closer to listen to the nun and Bienville, but his eyes never left the blonde's face. When she turned her head to speak with the person next to her, sunlight twisted and glinted in her honeyed hair. Its rich thickness enticed a man to plunge his fingers into its silky strands.

Though she wore a plain wool gown of blue with a simple ankle-length skirt, there was nothing plain about the way she carried herself. Rouen sensed she was out of place on a ship full of women bound for the New World to marry the colonists.

"We have your quarters ready at the fort, Sister Gertrude. I have planned a gathering for tomorrow night so the men can become acquainted with the women, if that meets with your approval."

"Tres bien, Governor Bienville."

Suddenly the blonde woman's gaze locked with Rouen's. The assessing boldness of her look made him smile, and he inclined his head toward her in a silent greeting. Wariness crept into her large brown eyes as they narrowed on him, and her mouth firmed into an impertinent line.

Their gazes remained bound, neither severing the visual contact until Bienville drew Rouen's attention by saying, "And, Sister Gertrude, this is Rouen Beauvoir. He has a large concession called Riverview not too far from the fort."

Rouen was forced to acknowledge the introduction, but the whole time he spoke to the nun, he felt the woman's stare on him. Throughout his life, he had been accustomed to automatic deference because of his position and family, but he sensed he would have to earn her respect, perhaps not an easy task.

As Sister Gertrude introduced each *casquette,* Rouen's gaze traveled down the line to rest upon the blonde with the dark, compelling eyes. The sea breeze continued playing with her hair, veiling her face. Absently she brushed away the strands, her gesture graceful, almost like a caress. Rouen sucked in a sharp breath, imagining those fingers touching him. He had been too long without a woman.

When the nun reached the lady with the honey-colored hair and said, "Danielle de Bussy," the woman met his look with an unwavering challenge of cool insolence.

While everyone else moved toward the fort, he and Danielle stood a few feet apart, staring at each other. Tension swirled about them like windblown sand. It vibrated from her as though she were trying to rein in her emotions and losing the battle.

"Your friends are leaving, *monsieur,*" Danielle murmured in a throaty voice, averting her gaze from his.

The corners of his mouth tilted upward; one thick eyebrow rose. " 'Tis true." He continued to block her way to the fort, trying to discern why Danielle de Bussy was among the others on *La Baleine.* Again he sensed this woman, who had climbed from the longboat to join the group with dignity and without fear in her eyes, didn't belong in the colony. "Allow me to escort you to Fort Louis."

She didn't reply, but instead swished around him to follow the group. Her head was held high, her poise unshaken as she started toward the unfinished fort.

Rouen shortened his long strides to walk beside Danielle. Their arms brushed. Slanting a look at her, he tried to fathom her reaction to the accidental touch. Her expression remained neutral, her gaze trained on the people in front of her as though he weren't beside her. But he also saw a slight tightening about her mouth.

"I trust your voyage was uneventful." Rouen broke the silence between them.

She stopped at the end of the pier. Turning to him, she said in that same throaty voice, "I am capable, *monsieur,* of following the party without assistance. You have better employment for your time, *non?*"

"My business is at the fort. We will walk together," he commanded, though his tone was quiet.

Dark fire flashed in her eyes. "I do not wish to walk with you." She whirled about and hurried after the party.

Chuckling, Rouen watched her until she caught up with the rest of the group. Feisty. Bold. He ran his hand along his jaw. Feeling the stubble of his beard, he realized he hadn't shaved before coming to the fort. He must be a sight with his buckskins, old and comfortably worn. He glanced down at the moccasins he wore and realized he looked more like a fur trapper than a gentleman. He strongly suspected her arrival in the New World was a shock to Mademoiselle Danielle de Bussy. She was no simple orphan raised by nuns.

At the entrance into the fort, she glanced back at him. An instant quickening shook the air, tilting the very ground he stood on. For a fleeting moment, he thought he saw a bruised expression in her eyes before she looked away and continued inside. He shook his head, trying to rid himself of the feeling of being denounced and appealed to at the same time.

After Bienville's party disappeared inside the unfinished log palisade, Rouen followed, turning his thoughts to his meeting with Delon. There was a disquieting tension in the air. He had felt it when he and Claude had gone on their scouting expedition to the wilderness inland two months before. Something was brewing in the colony.

Rouen retrieved his horse and started for home. The shadows of dusk fingered their way through the tall pine trees. The sound of his horse's hooves echoed through the forest, resounding through his mind as well. When he neared the stream, he scanned the terrain for any sign of Delon, but the man wouldn't make himself known until he thought they were safe and alone.

Out of the encroaching darkness came a rider. Rouen reined in Dancer and waited for Delon. They stood on the path, Delon's horse facing the opposite direction of Rouen's.

"I must be quick." The spy glanced about him, then continued, "Someone's inciting an Indian uprising against the French colonists. He's using English goods and weapons to entice the Indians."

"You did not learn his name?"

Delon shook his head, anger slashing across his mouth. "But I had to warn you to be careful. There have been reports of Chickasaw raiding parties farther south than usual. I'll be heading for the Mississippi soon to investigate rumors of the English approaching the Natchez Indians." He spurred his horse to a canter.

Like a kettle of water left on the fire to boil, it wouldn't be long until trouble exploded in the territory. Rouen frowned as he urged Dancer to a gallop through air laden with the tangy scents of sea and pine.

TWO

Beneath her drab wool skirt, Danielle tapped her foot impatiently, but not in time to the music being played for the gathering's enjoyment. She tried to tug her off-the-shoulder puffy sleeves up, but nothing she did changed the cut of her bodice, which revealed more than she wished.

She remembered once seeing a string of cattle being led to the slaughter. That was exactly how she felt. The three good sisters had led the women into this room, which she could tell served as a warehouse for supplies, with the intention of putting them on display for marriage. To Danielle, that meant the end of what little freedom she'd had since fleeing the Marquis. She didn't intend to go from one keeper to another.

Scanning the faces of the men in the room, she found Governor Bienville standing by Sister Gertrude. Danielle needed to speak with him. He might know where her uncle was. From the little she had been able to surmise earlier that day, her uncle wasn't living among the mass of people in the primitive conditions at Fort Louis.

As Danielle started toward Governor Bienville, Sister Gertrude stepped forward and the musicians stopped playing their violin, recorder, and bassoon. Everyone in the room fell silent. The nun went down the line, giving each woman's name, as the men on the other side of the room listened eagerly. Danielle's skin crawled as Sister Gertrude said her name. All eyes were on her. Again she wished her gown covered every inch of her body. Danielle tried to focus on a spot where the ceiling met the wall, but she couldn't help feeling like a piece of meat being inspected for consumption.

She hadn't realized she was holding her breath until Sister Gertrude finished and the noise level in the room rose. Slowly Danielle released her breath through pursed lips as the music began again.

"Did you see him?" Gaby asked excitedly.

"Who?" After the first day on the ship with Gaby, Danielle had given up trying to follow her friend's logic.

"Why, the man by the door, Danielle. Haven't you noticed him? He keeps staring at me. He's so huge and handsome." Gaby's blue eyes grew round. "He smiled at me!" She clutched Danielle's arm. "He's coming over here! What do I do?"

"Smile back." Danielle turned so she could see this man who so excited Gaby.

Briefly Danielle had wondered if Gaby had been referring to Rouen Beauvoir—huge and handsome described him well. His thick black hair, tied back in a ribbon, the cleft in his strong chin, his silver-gray eyes that glinted with humor, his full lips that curved up in an enticing smile haunted her more than she cared to acknowledge. Earlier she had been angry with herself when she had sought him out in the room full of men, but thankfully he hadn't been around when she had come in. She had no use for a man in her life.

The tall, powerfully built male, who wasn't Rouen, stopped in front of Gaby and bowed his head. "Allow me to introduce myself, *mademoiselle.* I'm Armand David." He lifted her hand—the one not clutching Danielle's arm for silent support—and kissed the back of it.

"Gabrielle Lavalle, Monsieur David." Gaby's hand slipped away from Danielle's arm.

Smiling, she turned away from the pair. She was happy for her friend. Armand David appeared to be better off than most in this room, and Danielle wished only good things for Gaby.

"Good evening, Mademoiselle de Bussy." A man of medium height, his mouth pinched, his blue eyes sharp, stood at her side.

Among the other men in the room he was overdressed in his frock coat of sky-blue satin, matching breeches, and peruke of powdered white hair. The lace cuffs of his shirt and jabot reminded Danielle of the Marquis, and she instantly recoiled.

"I'm Renaud Pinart."

He swept his arm across his body and bowed. The movement threw him off balance and he had to steady himself. When he tried to take her hand in his, she stubbornly kept her arms plastered to her sides.

"I have admired you from afar since yesterday when you landed," he slurred, his cold blue eyes becoming pinpoints as he inched closer to her, his breath reeking of alcohol. "Do you care to dance?"

She reacted to his nearness by backing away. It wasn't the ruffles or the fact that he was drunk that sickened her, it was his eyes. They looked so much like the Marquis's. There was no warmth in them, no life. She shivered and took another step away.

The smile that had never quite reached his eyes tensed in irritation. "I like spirit—to a point."

His hand snaked out to grab hers. Gasping at his quickness, she drew back and collided with someone. The solid muscles that pressed against her spine tightened; she smelled the familiar male scent of pine and leather and nearly sagged in relief.

"Danielle, you must forgive me. I fear I am late." The possessive ring to Rouen's words conveyed intimacy, as did the fact that he had placed his hands on her shoulders and pressed her back against him.

Pinart glanced from Danielle to Rouen to Danielle, the overdressed man's look frosty. With his jaw clamped shut, Pinart nodded curtly to the both of them, then stalked off.

Danielle tried to wrench free of Rouen's ironclad hold, but his fingers tightened on her shoulders. When she tried to tell him to take his hands off her, he murmured dangerously close to her ear, "Quiet, *ma petite.* Pinart is watching. Or would you rather I left you to him?"

"I can handle him," she whispered fiercely, wondering all the while if she could handle Rouen Beauvoir. "And I am not your little one. Me, I am not anyone's little one." Her father had called her that. Memories stirred in her mind of happy times when she had felt loved and protected. She could never allow herself to forget that wasn't her situation now. She could rely only on herself.

She slipped from his clasp only because he let her. Twisting about to face her rescuer, she schooled her features into an expressionless mask. "Though I am grateful for your knight errantry, I was about to lecture Monsieur Pinart on the art of gallantry."

Rouen's gray eyes glittered like polished silver caught in the sunlight. "That wouldn't have been wise, Mademoiselle de Bussy."

"The wisdom of my actions remains to be seen, since I was interrupted, *non?*" His eyes were so different from Pinart's. Rouen's were like fire and ice, never lifeless. Alarmed at her train of thought, she quickly said, "You will excuse me, *sil vous plait.* I've had enough of this—gathering."

"But, *mademoiselle,* you cannot leave." Rouen reached out to stop her.

She evaded his grasp, more because she didn't want to feel his hands on her traitorous body again than because he was trying to stop her from leaving. "But of course I shall leave if I want."

"No." His gaze drilled into hers as though he expected her to obey because he had commanded it.

"Non?" Anger at this man's audacity grew and raced through her bloodstream, becoming as much a part of her as her next heartbeat. She was through having a man tell her what to do.

"No, you don't, *mademoiselle.* It's not—"

With a calmness she didn't feel, she cut him off. "Perhaps you feel I should reward your gallantry. Me, I do not see it." Without another word, she spun about and stalked toward the door.

Outside, the cold winter night alleviated the heat of her anger—somewhat. She walked beside the building, trying to compose herself. She wouldn't leave until she talked with Governor Bienville, but she couldn't stay in that room with Rouen another moment.

She didn't like the way her heartbeat increased its pace or how her skin tingled when he looked at her in that particular way, his eyes singeing her, robbing her of her breath. He made her forget the purpose of her trip to the Louisiana Colony; he made her forget her plight and the Marquis. He was too dangerous. In her heart she knew that if her stepfather found her, she would become his prisoner—if he allowed her to live. But worst of all, she suspected Rouen Beauvoir could touch a part of her that she had locked away. To feel was to allow herself to be hurt.

She sensed his eyes on her before she found him in the shadows under the live oak. *"Monsieur,* you follow me? Why?"

Rouen didn't move from the darkness that cloaked him. "To protect you from yourself."

Her breath caught at the word *protect.* She was the only one she could depend on for her protection. That lesson had been hammered into her over the years with the Marquis.

Rouen stepped from the shadow of the tree. "There are very few women in the colony, Danielle. You shouldn't be alone out here in the dark. Some men take what they want without asking."

Her heart beat faster with each step he took toward her. "Are you one of those men?" she asked, upset that her voice sounded a shade unsure, a shade frightened.

"In some things, yes." He stopped not a foot from her. "I'm used to getting what I want."

His distinctive male scent engulfed her, inflaming

her senses. That scent had dwelled in her thoughts the day before like a warm memory. Suddenly she didn't want to run from him. There was a strength in him, but it wasn't threatening. He was very capable of protecting her, she realized with a jolt, and she had never had a true protector.

The idea was potent, tempting—for a brief span of time. In the end, she couldn't rely on him. She had trusted Pierre and he had betrayed that trust. She wouldn't make that mistake again.

"Why were you on *La Baleine?* I have observed you. This whole affair"—he gestured toward the building—"is distasteful to you."

"Do you know Monsieur Robert Havel?"

"I have heard of him. He married a Choctaw a few years back. They have a daughter."

"A Choctaw?"

"An Indian tribe that lives in these parts."

"This is not true," she murmured, startled at the news. Her uncle married to an Indian? Since arriving, she had heard stories about these Indians who lived in the New World that were frightening. Too much was happening in a short time. Her legs felt weak, and she wanted to steady herself before she did something foolish like collapse, but the nearest object to hold on to was Rouen.

"Without many white women in the colony, the men here often turn to the Indian women. Men get lonely and need—" His eyes, glinting with male interest, completed the sentence far more effectively than any words would.

Her thoughts raced with the added complication that her uncle had a family. That might change everything. "Where does he live?"

"Four days from here. I've passed by his cabin on two of my hunting trips and shared a drink with him."

"Then you know where it is," she whispered, more to herself than to him.

"Yes. Who is this Robert Havel to you?"

She stared into his face, the darkness hiding most of his expression from her view. But his confusion was a palpable force. "My uncle."

"Then you came here not to marry but to find your uncle?"

She had told no one her real motive for coming to the New World, but now there was no reason to stay silent. The nuns would find out soon enough when she refused anyone who asked for her hand in marriage. "Yes."

"Does Sister Gertrude know this?"

She shook her head.

"Does your uncle know you're here?"

"No."

"Do you have money to hire a guide to escort you to your uncle's?"

"No."

"Then how do you plan to get there?"

She breathed in deeply, releasing it slowly. "Will you escort me?" she blurted out, surprised at her bold question.

The air pulsated with his silence, and Danielle instantly regretted asking for his help. She would find the cabin by herself if need be, but one thing was for sure, she wouldn't stay here and marry a colonist.

"You're either very naive or desperate, Mademoiselle de Bussy. Which is it?"

His mockery incited her anger. She squared her shoulders and looked him straight in the eye. "Go to the devil, Monsieur Beauvoir."

Danielle started to storm away from him—something she seemed to do a lot around him—when his fingers closed around her arm, halting her. Rouen pulled her back, one arm encircling her to trap her against him. His free hand captured her chin and forced her to meet his gaze. She struggled to elude his grasp, but he tightened it.

He stared long and piercingly into her eyes. "You do not know me or what I'm capable of."

She knew that he was capable of making her forget the reason she was in the New World, that he was capable of making her body betray her mind. She was caught up in his keen regard, trying to deny what he was capable of and failing miserably.

"Do you know what it is like on the trail? We would be alone, miles from anybody else," he murmured in a husky voice, filled with raw passion.

Visions of them entwined together on a blanket invaded her mind, making her warm and tingling inside. Danielle inhaled a deep, bracing breath.

The slight movement of her chest against his ignited his desire, knotting the ache within him even tighter. Her nearness pushed logic from his mind as his hand slid into her silken hair to hold her head still while his mouth claimed hers. The grinding pressure of his lips quickly evolved into a tender persuasion, his tongue probing insistently, compelling her lips to part, to permit him entrance into her sweet cavern.

Danielle wanted to resist Rouen, to put an end to his kiss, but her body melted into his, her arms coming up to wind about him. His kiss deepened, sucking the very breath from her lungs. His large, rough hands stroked the length of her back—tender, gentle hands that seduced with an effectiveness hard to deny. Her world narrowed to the pleasure radiating from some hidden depth within her. She *needed* to break away before she felt possessed in every fiber of her being.

Danielle wedged her arms between them and shoved at his hard chest. Rouen drew his head back, but secured his arms about her waist. His gaze searched her features in the light of the half-moon.

"You win your point, *monsieur,*" she said in a shaky voice. "Release me immediately."

For a tension-fraught moment Danielle could feel the indecision in his body. Then, as suddenly as his kiss began, his arms dropped away from her. She staggered back.

"As you wish," Rouen murmured.

"I doubt you obey another's wishes unless you care to." She headed away from the building.

"Where are you bound, *mademoiselle?*"

She glanced back at him. "I shall retire for the night." When he advanced toward her, she hurriedly added, "It is my decision, *non?* You do not approve?" She shrugged. "I have the headache from all the—excitement this evening."

"Then I'll escort you."

"It would not help me to decline your escort?"

"You begin to understand me quite well."

His low chuckle danced along her spine, making her lengthen her stride. She couldn't wait to get inside the cabin. He was so exasperating, so infuriating—so tempting.

She hadn't intended to say another word to him, but at the door he took the matter into his own hands. She was positive he did that quite a lot. Rouen blocked her path, something in his stance as untamed and fierce as the wilderness about them. Every hard line in his tall, intimidating bearing could only be interpreted as dangerous to her peace of mind.

"Surely you will not retire without bidding me good night, *mademoiselle.* After all, I may have saved you from . . . God knows what."

"Monsieur?" Her brown eyes widened in mock confusion.

He waved his hand toward the blackness. "Who knows what lurked there, waiting for you."

"Perhaps the only danger stands before me, *non?*"

He bridged the short distance between them until his breath mingled with hers. His forceful presence overwhelmed her. At five-feet-nine, she was tall for a woman, but Rouen was at least a half a foot taller.

Though he wore an elegant, full-cut coat of midnight blue velvet, a thigh-length waistcoat of brocade silk, and a stock of white muslin, underneath he was muscular, powerful. Part of his dark hair curled in a tangle of disorder about his strong features; the rest was secured in a queue. His chiseled cheekbones accentuated his ruggedness, italicizing the bronze cast of his skin. Rouen Beauvoir was elemental and masterful, a man who controlled his own destiny, a man to avoid. He could suck the life from her, making her forget everything.

"Monsieur Beauvoir, I'm tired. I've been on a horrible ship for weeks. At times I wondered if we would make it to this place." Her voice manifested all her confused exhaustion.

He curved his hand along the side of her face. "Then I bid you good night, Danielle."

His mouth slowly descended toward hers. She felt transfixed, as though she were watching this scene from afar. Her lips tingled in anticipation; her body involuntarily arched toward him.

A sound penetrated her dazed mind and broke through the sensual spell, dispersing it on the sea-laced breeze. Stunned at her response to Rouen, afraid of the power he exerted so effortlessly, Danielle backed away, spinning about to return to the gathering where there were people.

Out of the dark trees, a figure lurched toward her, colliding with her. The man grabbed at her, trying to keep himself from falling. Before she could do anything, he slid down her length and collapsed to the ground. Everything happened so fast that Danielle didn't even have time to scream. As she stared at the man at her feet, blood gushed from a wound in his chest. The crimson pool sparkled in the moonlight. A scream welled up inside her.

Rouen's hand clamped about her mouth. "Don't, Danielle."

The urgency in his words frightened her even more, but she nodded her understanding. His hand slipped away and he knelt beside the man.

"Delon?"

The wounded man tried to grasp Rouen's coat, but lacked the strength. Rouen leaned closer as the man whispered, "Traitor among us." He coughed, blood trickling from his mouth. "Guard your—"

The man went limp, his lifeless eyes staring straight ahead.

Paralyzed with shock, Danielle didn't realize that Rouen had risen and was speaking to her until he clasped her arms and shook her.

"Danielle! Come on."

Rouen led her toward the cabin. At the door, he fumbled for the latch, and she freed herself from his hold. Swinging around, she pointed at the man on the ground, her hand trembling. "What about him? You cannot leave him there."

"I won't. But first I want you inside. Then I will go for Governor Bienville. You needn't get involved in this."

"Why did he warn you?" Danielle asked as Rouen opened the door.

"This is the wilderness. There are men here who will kill without thought. Now do you understand why you must have an escort even here at the fort?" His words were sharper than he had intended, but Delon's murder implied the traitor knew who Delon was. He might also know who Rouen was. The traitor was obviously a Frenchman.

While Rouen lit a candle, Danielle stood in the center of the main room, trying to regain control. Her body shook with the memory of seeing the man die at her feet. She had never seen anyone die—certainly never witnessed a murder. The emotional trauma of the evening took its toll; exhaustion wove through her body. This shock, piled on top of all the others, threatened her equilibrium.

When Rouen finally looked at her in the candlelight, his gaze shifted to her gown. Danielle glanced down and gasped. Her blue dress was covered with the murdered man's blood.

"*Mon Dieu!* I—" Words failed her as she stared at the dark red stain.

"Danielle, go and change!"

Rouen's stern words drove into her, demanding her attention. Her gaze lifted and clashed with his. A band of anguish tightened about her chest, making breathing difficult.

"Now, Danielle. I will await you outside." There was a tenderness in his gray eyes as he took in her pale features.

She shook her head. "I'm fine." When he cocked an eyebrow, she added, "You must report this to Governor Bienville. He will find the killer, *non?* Perhaps he is still in the fort—" Panic inched into her voice, contradicting her earlier words. "What if the killer is still here?" Shudder after shudder slithered down her spine. She hugged her arms to her as cold embedded itself in the marrow of her bones.

"Whoever did it will have fled." In three long strides, Rouen stood before her, his presence a comfort she wished she could deny. "Even so, Danielle, bolt the door after I leave."

She nodded, unable to speak, her throat tight with emotions that threatened what little composure she had left. His gentle hands cradled her face, his restraint stressed by the muscles that corded and tensed on his arms.

"You will be all right?"

She stepped away from his touch. Assembling the scattered fragments of her poise, she finally answered, "Yes. Go. Do what you must. I'll be all right."

She had survived an attempted rape by the Marquis and a harrowing journey on *La Baleine;* she would survive the horror of seeing a man die. She had no choice. In the past months, she had learned that to survive meant to shut off her emotions. She would survive to repay the Marquis for his cruelties to her and her mother. She had only one purpose: to return to France someday and make the Marquis pay.

Rouen hesitated, as though he debated between believing her and staying. "Remember, bolt the door."

"I will."

He waited outside until he heard the bolt slide into place before heading to inform Governor Bienville of Delon's murder. Inside the meeting hall, Rouen quickly found the governor in a discussion with several planters.

"I need to speak with you in private." Rouen kept his voice level, his expression blank. He didn't want everyone at the gathering to know about Delon's murder. He wanted to discover how much Bienville knew about Delon's connection to the Minister of Finance.

"You wish to ask for Mademoiselle de Bussy's hand? You must speak to Sister Gertrude. Have a care, Rouen. Your father would be unhappy if you married that woman. She's beautiful, *oui,* and has a certain appeal, but—"

"Jean-Baptiste!"

"I err, *mon ami?*"

"Monsieur Delon has been murdered. I found his body while walking Mademoiselle de Bussy home." Rouen studied the governor.

"Murdered? I met Delon once or twice, but I didn't know him. Where's his body?"

Rouen left the meeting hall with Governor Bienville, satisfied the man wasn't aware of Delon's spying. The fewer people who knew about Delon, the better it would be. Right now he trusted no one, not even the governor. Delon had said there was a traitor among them, and obviously Delon had been right.

An hour later, Rouen had finished his explanations and the uproar over Delon's murder had diminished among those at the gathering. In the meeting hall, Rouen scanned the familiar faces in the crowd, trying to determine who was the killer. He had purposely lied earlier to Danielle about the man being gone from the fort because he didn't want her to worry. Instinct told him the murderer was standing in the room with him, possibly even watching him, waiting for the right moment.

The murder added an excitement to the gathering. Disgusted, Rouen made his way toward the door. He would check on Danielle, then return to Riverview.

When he knocked on her door and no one answered, he became worried. Pounding his fist into the wood, he was preparing to break into the cabin when Danielle slid back the bolt and let him inside.

"You should have asked who it was," Rouen immediately commanded, noting the blanket she must have hastily grabbed to cover herself. "I could have been the murderer." The sharpness left his voice as his gaze roamed down the length of her, his desire rekindled.

"Only one person in this fort would pound the

door so impatiently," she retorted, disconcerted by the look in his eyes.

He leaned against the jamb, his loose-jointed stance belying the seduction of his survey. "I wanted to inform you that all has been taken care of."

"Thank you," she murmured, her gaze drawn to his like the sea to the shore. She tightened the blanket about her, but nothing could shield her from his male regard. She felt assessed, probed, on display more than when she had been introduced to the men of the fort. Her cheeks flamed.

"You are sure you're all right?"

His husky voice sent a tingle down her spine. No, she wasn't all right as long as he stood a foot from her with a look that could devour her. "What did Governor Bienville say when you reported the murder?"

"He will look into it, but his resources are limited." Rouen moved closer and lowered his voice. "You needn't worry about anyone knowing of your involvement. I led them to believe I found Delon already dead."

Danielle could smell his distinctive scent and found herself distracted by his nearness. She stepped back to give herself some space. How could she forget that a man died at her feet, muttering a warning to Rouen? She forced herself to focus on what they were discussing, to ignore how her pulse raced at his nearness. "The man knew you. He was warning you about . . . something."

"As I said, this is a rugged place."

"No, it was more than that. You are in danger."

He smiled, reaching out and brushing his fingers

down the side of her face. "Your tender regard honors me."

She jerked back from the contact with his fingers, but their rough feel still lingered on her cheek. "I know you too little to honor you."

"That can change."

"It is possible, *monsieur,* but I do not plan to be here forever."

"Good night, Danielle."

The caress of her name on his lips sent a delicious sensation to her feminine core, mocking her earlier protest. Her staccato heartbeat rendered her weak and made her legs tremble. She held onto the door to steady herself. "Good night."

They stared at each other for a long moment, both silent. Then Danielle closed the door and locked it. Rouen waited a minute longer, imagining her slipping off the blanket and lying down on her pallet. His groin ached as he shook the image from his mind and walked to his horse, frustrated and confused by his attraction to her.

By her own words she had traveled to the Louisiana Colony not to marry but to find her uncle. Bienville was right about his father's reaction if he wed someone of Danielle's station. She wanted everyone to believe she was a maiden of uncertain background raised in a convent. As he recited all the reasons not to be attracted to her, he knew he wouldn't listen to his common sense. He would be back tomorrow to see Danielle de Bussy. She offered him a challenge he found hard to resist.

The overhanging branches of the large oaks along the path to Riverview dripped with gray-green moss, casting eerie ghosts in the moonlight that filtered through the trees. In the distance, an owl sought its prey. Rouen tried to remain alert as he rode toward his plantation, but thoughts of Danielle diverted his attention. She was an enigma, riddled with puzzles and conflicting emotions, a woman in transition. He had always been attracted to a mystery. She dared him to discover the true woman beneath the mistrust, loneliness, and, he believed, vulnerability. Someone had hurt her badly. That impression was indelible—the way she bore herself proudly, apart from others, but with a touch of raw emotions not quite concealed.

A sound disintegrated the vision, alerting him to danger. Before he could react, a body crashed into his, knocking him off his horse.

THREE

Rouen and his attacker slammed into the hard ground. The breath-wrenching impact stunned Rouen. For a few precious seconds his mind clouded and blackness threatened to swallow him. He shook his head hard to clear it while he tried to push off his heavier attacker. The man's large, beefy arms tightened.

He rolled over and over, trying to throw off the attacker. Willing a super strength into his arms, Rouen finally broke the ironclad hold about him and shoved off his attacker's massive bulk. Scrambling to his feet, Rouen distanced himself from the larger man.

The moonlight cast the man's features in sinister shadows, making his face a deadly mask. Rouen crouched low, arms outstretched, feet braced apart, weight evenly distributed to ensure he could move at a second's notice in either direction. He knew his only hope was his quickness, because the man before him held a knife in one hand and outweighed him by a good thirty pounds.

So intent was Rouen on his attacker and the knife that it took him several seconds to realize that another man was dismounting and joining his friend.

Rouen slanted a look at Dancer. He had a long knife secured to his saddle. If he could maneuver himself nearer to his stallion, he might have a chance against the two ruffians.

With a quickness that took both men by surprise, Rouen lunged for Dancer. He unsheathed his knife and rounded on his attackers, who started for him, then halted when they saw the metal gleam.

For a silent moment Rouen sized up the situation while the two men did likewise. Rouen knew he might not survive their assault. If not, he was damned sure going to go down fighting, hopefully taking one with him. Questions shot through his mind as he shifted his knife to his right hand, readying himself for their attack. Were these two men Delon's murderers? If so, who sent them after him? They weren't the masterminds behind the English plot; all they had going for them was brute strength.

A look passed between the two men. The smaller one backed away, allowing the large man, who reminded Rouen of a brown bear, to face him alone. "Ya can't fight us both, so why don't ya gives it up? We ain't goin' t' hurt ya."

Rouen laughed, a bone-chilling sound that would have made any sane man pause. He didn't reply, but his body tensed as he mentally prepared himself for the man's first move. It came a split second later. The bear-like attacker flew at Rouen, his knife driving toward Rouen's chest. The second man skirted Rouen and disappeared. Rouen quickly sidestepped the large ruffian's thrust as he plunged his own knife toward the soft flesh of the man's stomach.

His blade grazed his attacker's side. Suddenly the second man pinned Rouen from behind.

Enraged, Rouen twisted and fought to free his arms. The large man, grimacing in pain, stepped in front of Rouen and raised his hand. The man's fist connected with Rouen's jaw, and his head reeled back from the powerful blow. The strong stench of alcohol clouded his senses. A dark void lurked at the edges of his mind. Another strike at his face drove the blissful blackness closer as Rouen struggled to retain consciousness. Again and again, he was hammered with punches to the face and stomach. Blackness descended . . .

Pinpricks of consciousness jabbed into Rouen's mind, demanding that he feel the pain throbbing through him, that he awaken from his dark haven. For a moment, he wondered why he was still alive—he hurt too much to be dead—then decided it didn't matter why as long as he used it to his advantage and paid his two attackers back for every painful punch.

Slowly words penetrated his mind, and he became alert to what the two men were talking about. Lying perfectly still, with his eyes closed, Rouen listened.

" 'Tis the easiest damned money we've made in a long time."

Rouen didn't have to look to know that the bearlike attacker spoke. His voice boomed through the stillness of the night. Rouen's body grew taut at his boasting. It took a great deal of willpower not to show that he had regained consciousness. Again he wondered who had paid the men to assault him.

"We've not got him t' the boat yet."

" 'Twon't be no problem. He's trussed up like a damn pig 'bout t' be roasted. He ain't goin' nowheres."

"Louie, we weren't t' hurt him! What in the hell got into your thick skull?"

"Ya worry too damned much, Gustave. By the time he's in France, all the bruises will be healed."

Rouen clamped his jaws so tightly that pain bolted down his neck. He remembered the sadistic pleasure the bear-like man had taken while beating him up. Then all at once the meaning of the words sank in. France? Who was after him in France?

"Ya idiot! He can talk, and rest assured he will. We mightn't receive the money owed us."

"Ya held him!" Louie shouted.

Rouen could picture the bear-like man leaping to his feet and preparing to do battle with his cohort. Rage trembled through the man's words. A sane person would be leery of angering him.

A short bark of laughter pierced the air. "Oh, was I s'pose t' let him go an' get himself kilt by ya in a knife fight?"

Rouen viewed the pair by the fire through slitted eyes. They were oblivious to him as they faced each other, the blaze between them molding their features in a golden-red hue. It reminded him of the flames of hell. He hoped they took care of each other and saved him the trouble.

For a long moment, the pair scowled at each other over the fire. Then the smaller man shrugged, turned away from the bear-like man, and murmured, "Ain't no use us fightin' over dis. We've gots him an' soon the Duc de Beauvoir will pay us for deliverin' him. I gots my share spent."

In the dark shadows Rouen stiffened at his father's name. No wonder he hadn't received another letter. His father had taken the matter into his own hands, as usual. Anger vibrated through Rouen, threatening his ruse of unconsciousness. He forced himself to breathe deeper, but the blood that coursed through his veins was hotter than the fire ten feet away.

"We'd better sleep if we're goin' t' make the ship on the morrow," the man named Gustave said. "Check our guest t' make sure he don't go nowheres."

"Sure. Me pleasure."

As Louie approached him, Rouen relaxed his body, every muscle limp. The man jerked on the ropes that bound Rouen's wrists and feet. The hemp dug into his skin, but he remained quiet, his mind already beginning to work on a plan of escape. He had no intention of going back to France until he was ready, and then only on his terms.

"Tied neat an' pretty," the bear-like man called back to his companion.

Rouen waited half an hour before he opened his eyes a fraction to see if the men were asleep. Both were sprawled out by the fire, the huge man's snores vying with the sounds of the night. Rouen wasted no more time. He began to work the rope loose. An hour later, the hemp slipped from his wrists, and he quickly untied the one about his feet.

Crouching, he surveyed the scene before him, trying to decide the best course of action. His fury toward his father still threatened his logical side. In the years he had been in the colony, he had become his own man. He would never give that up, even when he returned to France.

His eyes lit upon the larger man. Rouen's smile would have chilled the man if he had been awake. Quietly, like an Indian stealing through the forest, Rouen made his way to the man and hit him over the head with a nearby rock.

After binding Louie's hands, Rouen then proceeded to Gustave, sliding the knife he had retrieved over the man's throat. A thin line of blood appeared. Gustave's eyes popped open.

"*Bonsoir* or should I say *bonjour?*" Rouen smiled, a cold uplifting of the corners of his mouth. He could smell the man's fear.

Gustave opened his mouth to speak, but Rouen pressed the knife into his flesh. "Silence! I have a message for the Duc de Beauvoir. Tell him if he tries this again, I'll never return to France, title or no title." He lessened the pressure on the man's throat and added, "If you're smart, you'll deliver the message. I don't take kindly to being crossed."

Gustave nodded, his eyes wide with terror, sweat beading his forehead.

"*Bien.* We understand each other, then." Before the man could react, Rouen struck him with his fist. The sound echoed in the clearing.

He used the rest of the pair's rope to tie up Gustave, then hauled the bear-like man to a horse and heaved him up onto the animal's back. Rouen didn't want to leave both men together. He would deposit the larger one with Governor Bienville.

On the short ride back to the fort, Rouen's emotions catapulted through a wide range of feelings toward his father. Finally indifference settled over him as he tied his horse to the post in front of Bienville's house. He realized if he allowed his true feelings to take root, he was afraid of what he would do. He had learned long ago that indifference was the only way to handle his domineering father.

As dawn filtered through the clouds, a cold, damp chill lingered in the air. Rouen pounded on Bienville's thick wooden door, glancing back once to see if Louie was still unconscious. At the sight of the large man lying sprawled over his horse's back, Rouen rubbed his sore jaw, wincing at the pain that bolted down his neck when he touched it.

The door swung open to reveal Solomon. Rouen stepped through the entrance, saying, "I must see Governor Bienville. Is he up yet?"

"He's dressing, 'Sieur Beauvoir."

"Please inform him I'm here. I'll wait for him in his office." With the familiarity of a good friend, Rouen headed to the governor's office, where he could keep an eye on his captive in front of the house.

Five minutes later Bienville joined him, concern on his face. "Solomon was right—you look much the worse for wear."

Rouen glanced down at his fine evening clothes, now torn and dirty, and laughed. "I feel as bad as I look."

"What happened?" Bienville settled into his chair by the fireplace.

As Rouen half-leaned, half-sat on the governor's desk, he told his friend about the attack, leaving out the part concerning his father. He didn't want Bienville caught in the battle of wills between them. The

Duc de Beauvoir was a powerful man in France, someone even Bienville in the New World shouldn't cross.

"And you say the man who attacked you is outside?"

Rouen nodded. "There is a boat leaving for the river later today?"

"Yes."

"Perhaps this man could benefit you as a laborer at Nouvelle Orleans. He can probably lift twice the weight of a normal man. It'll do the brute good to toil in the swamps for a while."

"You don't wish me to detain him in our lovely fort?"

"No. I think this will teach him a lesson he won't forget." Besides, Rouen didn't want Bienville questioning Louie and discovering who paid him. The governor would urge Rouen to return to France immediately, and he wasn't ready to do that.

"Then I'll have Solomon deliver the man to the captain."

Rouen pushed himself away from the desk and shook Bienville's hand. "I don't care to live my life looking over my shoulder."

"Do you suppose this man murdered Devon last night?"

"No."

"So positive, Rouen?" Bienville's eyes narrowed on his friend.

"Instinct, Jean-Baptiste. Instinct." Rouen walked toward the door.

"A word of advice, *mon ami.* My instinct tells me you should watch your back. I've known you long enough to suspect you're into something that isn't safe."

Rouen gestured toward the window. "As you see, I take care of myself."

"Even a cat's nine lives run out."

Rouen left the governor's house more troubled than he let his friend know. He stared across the compound toward Danielle's cabin. With determination in his long strides, he headed toward it to see Danielle.

Sister Gertrude was surprised to find such an early morning visitor, especially one who looked so disheveled, but after Rouen gave her a persuasive smile and a brief explanation, she let him inside and went to fetch Danielle.

Rouen paced back and forth, running his fingers through his hair repeatedly. He should leave before she came. He wasn't even sure why he was visiting Danielle so quickly after last night, like some eager suitor. When he heard footsteps, he halted in the middle of the room and turned toward the entrance.

Danielle paused in the doorway, her eyes growing round as she took in the appalling appearance of Rouen Beauvoir, his elegant clothes ruined, his face cut and bruised. He probably had gotten drunk after he left her the night before, then had become involved in a brawl. He was no different than other men. She had spent a restless night dreaming of him, and now was angry with herself for wasting a moment's sleep. "*Monsieur,* you did not return home last night?"

"No, I was detained."

"Do you make it a practice to pay your morning

calls dressed like—like this?" She waved her hand toward his attire. Since her arrival, she had seen evidence of violence everywhere.

"Perhaps my attire offends you?"

"Our butler would have turned you from the door." Danielle started to say more, then realized she had said too much.

"Ah, of course. The butler at the convent?"

"It is of no concern to you, *monsieur.*"

He shrugged, turning away from her. "What can you expect from a heathen?"

His words mocked her, but they also made clear to Danielle how alien the world was that she had thrust herself into to escape her stepfather. "I can see, not much," she retorted, focusing on Rouen's image now, rather than the disturbing Rouen, who had played across her mind during the night. "Why am I so honored by your visit?" Her question rivaled his earlier tone of mockery.

He pivoted toward her, his slate gray eyes intent on her face. "I have decided to offer you my services as an escort."

"C'est vrai? But, *non,* I must decline." She stayed in the doorway of the two-room cabin, needing to keep as much distance between them as possible.

His gray eyes darkened like clouds gathering for a storm. "Mine is the best offer you will receive."

Danielle desperately tried to come up with a logical reason to refuse him. "As you made clear last night, I cannot pay you."

"My services are free."

Her heart pounded against her breast. "Nothing is free."

"Cynicism in one so young?"

"Age has naught to do with experience."

He cocked his head to one side, studying her. "A woman raised in a convent? What would you know of experience?" The lift of one black eyebrow italicized the fact he didn't believe her story, that she was hiding from something or someone.

"Sister Mary Catherine believed in a complete education. I know—" Her words trailed off into silence. She had been about to tell this stranger that she knew what transpired between a man and a woman and wanted nothing to do with it.

He smiled, a slow, melting smile that transformed his roughened features into a sensual countenance. "You know *what,* Danielle?"

Her gaze slid to the wooden floor between them. "Me, I know about economy. A person is to be paid for service rendered." She stabbed him with a withering look. "And I have no money, as you so kindly pointed out last night, Monsieur Beauvoir. So what do you expect as payment?" She was determined to put the conversation between them on a formal basis.

"If you're worried about your virtue, you needn't be. I would never touch you—unless you wanted me to."

She drew herself up straight, proud. "Never."

His smile faded. Why in the hell was he arguing with this woman? If he were smart, which he was beginning to doubt, he would leave at a gallop and never return. But he knew he wouldn't. For some strange reason, he felt responsible for Danielle. If he deposited her with her uncle, surely that feeling would abate. Raking his hand through his hair in exasperation, he asked in the most patient voice he could muster, "Then what will you do, Mademoiselle de Bussy?"

"I—" What would she do? She would be confined to this fort unless she found a way to travel safely to her uncle's. She would never find her uncle's place by herself. The New World was too different from France. It was wide open spaces with large forests and swamps in between. A person could travel for miles and miles and never see a living soul. The night before, she had even heard men talking about Indians, savages with red skin, fierce warriors who lived in the colony. Reluctantly she admitted to herself that she did need a guide.

Rouen folded his arms across his chest, his gray eyes gleaming with amusement. "Well?"

"Well!" She drew in a deep, fortifying breath. "I have no other choice yet, *monsieur.* That pleases you, *non?*"

"It depends. Do you wish my escort or not?"

"Why are you so eager, Monsieur Beauvoir?"

That was a good question. Why was he insisting? He wanted to believe he needed to get away from the area until it was safer for him. But that was a lie. He was attracted to Danielle. It was that simple and yet that complicated, too. "Business demands I travel inland."

Danielle realized that Monsieur Beauvoir was her best chance of getting to her uncle's safely, yet she hesitated. She had a hard time trusting anyone. Worse, she didn't trust *herself* around the man.

Rouen covered the distance between them quickly. "I won't offer a second time."

The steel in his voice warned her she was allowing her only possibility to slip away, but she didn't want to be backed into a corner. She felt trapped by his virile nearness and wished she could escape. Stepping to the side, she attempted to put some space between them, but his arm shot out and stopped her. His other captured her effectively against the wall beside the door. Though he was close, his body didn't touch hers, but Danielle could smell the male scent of pine. She trained her gaze on the cleft in his chin, trying to avoid looking into his piercing eyes.

"Are you afraid of me, *mademoiselle?*"

Her gaze slowly traveled upward, taking in his swollen lips, cut now into a frown; his strong jawline, bruised, covered in a day's growth of black beard; his storm gray eyes. "You yourself cautioned me last night about men taking what they wanted without asking." She strove to keep her voice calm while her heart sprinted faster.

He leaned closer. "I told you I never take without permission, *mademoiselle.*"

She swallowed hard. "I do not understand. Why else should you bother to escort me?"

"You think I cannot gain your acquiescence?" he taunted, shoving himself back a step.

She straightened, her chin tilted at a challenging angle. "No!"

"Then you need not worry. Nor need you persuade me from my good deed." His voice sounded bored and his look was neutral as it brushed over her. "Your answer, *mademoiselle.* I grow impatient to be on my way. As you can see, I must bathe and change clothing."

Involuntarily her gaze roamed down the muscled length of him, taking in his torn, dirty attire. "What happened? Someone took umbrage with your arrogance, *non?*" she asked, wanting to confirm for her peace of mind how barbaric he was. It would help her to keep her distance.

"Nothing of importance," he answered, impatience lacing his voice. He needed to get away from her before he went back on his word and did something without her permission. He was too tired and sore to fight the male urges that came to the foreground around this woman. If she refused his offer, he needn't worry how he was going to keep from touching her on the trail. If she accepted . . . "*Mademoiselle,* your answer?"

"Yes."

With that one word, a door closed on a trap Rouen had set himself. He nodded curtly and headed for the front door. "Be ready tomorrow at dawn."

Framed in the entrance, Danielle watched Rouen mount his horse and ride away. Her emotions flitted from excitement to bewilderment to apprehension. Apprehension won out. She would be alone with him for days in the wilderness, miles from the nearest person. Whatever possessed her to think this man would be civil? Whatever possessed her to agree to the trip?

Sinking down onto a bench in front of the hearth, Danielle tried to list all the reasons she needed Rouen Beauvoir in order to be safe from her stepfather. But an image of Rouen—shirtless, his booted feet planted slightly apart, his black hair tousled by the wind, his eyes hungrily devouring her—nudged its way into her mind, chasing away any peace she might have at the knowledge she would soon find her uncle and have a loved one as a protector against the Marquis—that she finally wouldn't be alone in her battle against her stepfather.

FOUR

The leering face of the Marquis filled Danielle's dreams. He thrust his face into hers, his eyes glinting with desire as he tied her to the bed, his captive. He stripped off his clothes, and laughter exploded from his mouth as shock and horror transformed her angry expression.

"You can't escape me. You'll always be mine," he announced triumphantly, kneeling on the bed between her spread legs. "And now I'll take you. No man will want you again."

As he lowered himself toward her, Danielle bolted upright on her crude pallet. Sweat drenched her body; her breath came in gasps. It took her a few minutes to realize she wasn't at Chateau Duchamp but in the Louisiana Colony. She was safe—for now.

Not even in her sleep could she escape the Marquis. He had tormented her the whole journey, as if he were there beside her, taking sadistic pleasure in her anguish.

He would pay for what he had done to her and her mother, Danielle swore. For the past ten years, their life had been a living hell. Witnessing her mother's humiliation day after day at the hands of the Marquis made Danielle resolve never to let a man rule her life. She would answer only to herself from now on.

"Did you have another nightmare?" Gaby sat up next to Danielle.

"He comes closer. I'm afraid one day I won't wake up before he—" Shuddering, Danielle tried not to think about the nightmare. She had told Gaby about the dream after she had awakened with a cry the first night on the ship. She had never told Gaby, though, who the man in the nightmare was.

"Those dreams will go away when you find a husband who will take care of you and protect you. He'll make you forget."

Never! "Perhaps you speak the truth, Gaby."

"Oh, I can't wait till I marry." She bent closer to Danielle and lowered her voice to a whisper. "I have a confession to make. I hated living in a convent. 'Twas so—quiet."

Danielle laughed. Her friend loved to talk. In fact, the nuns had shortened her name from Gabrielle to Gaby, she had informed Danielle the first day they met, because she talked when she was supposed to be silent.

"Have you ever thought about the man you'll marry?"

Instantly Rouen's taunting face intruded into Danielle's mind. "No," she answered, perturbed at her traitorous thoughts.

"I have. I've never had anything of my own. When we marry, we'll be the mistresses of our own homes."

More likely slaves to our husbands, Danielle thought. She kept that opinion to herself.

"I will talk when I want, leave the house when I want."

If your husband permits it. Danielle could never forget how restricted her mother's life was at the chateau.

"I hope my husband is tall, handsome, and rich," Gaby whispered.

"In the wilderness?"

Gaby giggled. "Well, I would settle for taller than me with his own house for us to live in."

Two nights before, Danielle had seen a man die at her feet. She had listened to the other women wailing their misery as the sea tossed the ship about. She would settle for nothing less than revenge against the Marquis, Danielle declared silently, and felt her hatred grow as she looked about at the crude place where they were housed—a log cabin inside an unfinished fort.

Restless, she rose and walked to the hearth that barely warmed the room. The gray ashes in the grate reminded her of Rouen's eyes when she had not accepted his offer immediately.

Rouen Beauvoir was a man who got his own way. She doubted women denied him anything. From the way he held his head to the intimidating set of his shoulders to the sinewy power of his legs, he exuded sexuality. She hadn't been able to sleep very well in anticipation of the journey into the wilderness, for fear of weakening toward Rouen.

This trip wasn't wise. She felt it deep inside. And yet she had no choice. Rouen was the best person to guide her to her uncle's. She believed him when he said he wouldn't harm her. But though she trusted him to a point, she wondered if she trusted herself around him. His nearness did strange things to her insides, turning them all hot and liquid, sensations she didn't understand—sensations she didn't want to experience.

"Danielle?"

She offered her friend a tentative smile that almost instantly disappeared as she bent and retrieved her blue wool gown from the small trunk the nuns had supplied for her few possessions.

"I've been excited 'bout this journey from the beginning, but you have not." Gaby glanced at the other three women, who still slept. "You do not intend to marry, *oui?*"

Danielle shook her head, then slipped the gown over her shift, lacing the bodice in front. "I needed to travel to my uncle's, and a woman traveling alone isn't safe. Sister Mary Catherine at the convent where I was raised thought this was the best way." The lie came easily to her lips now, something else she had to thank the Marquis for. Honesty was important to her, and she didn't like living a lie.

Gaby came toward her. "Then why are you upset now? Monsieur Beauvoir is escorting—" She laughed, slapping her forehead with the heel of her hand. "Ah, I see. Your restless nights are caused by Monsieur Beauvoir, *oui?*"

Danielle started to deny it, but Gaby interrupted. "Of course, I don't blame you for being disturbed by him. He's"—she searched for the right words—"so powerful."

"He affects me not. I'm concerned about the journey itself. I'm not used to the wilderness and these people called Indians. The stories I've heard frighten me."

"Is it the stories that frighten you or the feelings Monsieur Beauvoir creates? After he left yesterday, all you did was brood, hardly saying two words to any of us. When you told Sister Gertrude about your trip and she became so upset, nothing seemed to fret you. I thought Sister Gertrude would faint."

"But Governor Bienville informed her that Monsieur Beauvoir was above reproach and a perfect escort for me."

"Yes, but he had to be very, very persuasive with Sister Gertrude, that one." Gaby's blue eyes shone with amusement. "She takes her duties quite seriously, does she not? I do believe she had several prospective grooms for you."

Danielle shivered, a picture of her mother at the mercy of the Marquis pervading her thoughts. "I will wed no one!"

Gaby's eyes dilated in surprise; she threw a nervous glance toward the other women to make sure they were still asleep. "But what else is there?"

"I—" Danielle could come up with nothing else. All her life she had been trained to be a wife and run a large household. In frustration she finally declared, "I will think on it."

"Well, I want a husband. I want children."

"Have you a husband in mind?" Danielle wanted to change the subject because she, too, would love to have children, but that took a husband.

A smile dimpled Gaby's cheeks. "Most definitely. Monsieur David."

The sound of footsteps approaching prevented Danielle from commenting on Gaby's choice. Danielle quickly finished dressing, putting on her stockings and shoes as Sister Gertrude bustled into the room.

"Danielle, I hope you slept well. Governor Bienville told me it's a long, hard journey to your uncle's."

"I'm fine, Sister Gertrude. I awakened early because I'm excited. I haven't seen Uncle Robert in years."

The nun's chest heaved in a long sigh. "I dislike your traveling alone with Monsieur Beauvoir."

"But Governor Bienville spoke very highly of him." Danielle had gone over this very subject the evening before with the nun.

"I know. I know." Sister Gertrude placed her hands on her hips, chewing on her bottom lip as she silently debated something with herself. Finally, in a huff, she said, "But a man can forget he's a gentleman when there's no one around to remind him."

Danielle doubted Rouen had ever been a complete gentleman. Underneath his polished charm was an untamed primitiveness that intrigued her as well as scared her. She was sure Monsieur Beauvoir could protect her, even from the Indians. Physically she would be in no danger. Emotionally, perhaps not. She must fight harder to control her feelings. Focusing her thoughts and energy on her stepfather would help.

When Monsieur Beauvoir knocked at the front door, Danielle's heartbeat began to speed. Moistening her lips nervously, she wiped her sweaty palms on the drab wool of her gown, squared her shoulders, and walked toward the door with her small trunk of worldly goods—one change of clothing.

She was using Monsieur Beauvoir to accomplish the last leg of a long journey. That was the only reason he was important to her, she told herself as she pulled the door open.

The man standing before her wasn't Monsieur Beauvoir. He was a stranger of medium height, dressed in buckskins and a fur cap, with an array of features toughened by the sun and harsh conditions in the colony. Danielle couldn't take her eyes off the long red scar down one side of his face that distorted the rest of his features.

Claude removed his fur cap. "Mademoiselle de Bussy, I'm Claude Renoir. Monsieur Beauvoir sent me to fetch you. He needed to see the governor before leaving." When Danielle didn't reply but continued to stare at him, he added in an uncomfortable voice, "I'll be traveling with you to your uncle's."

Danielle snapped out of her daze. She had been expecting to face Rouen and had prepared herself for it. Claude Renoir's appearance had thrown her off guard. "You'll be going with us?"

Claude winced at the shocked tone of her voice. "Yes."

She wouldn't be alone with Rouen for the next four days. A smile of relief touched her lips. "I'm glad." She turned and hugged Gaby and Sister Gertrude good-bye. "Don't worry about me. You see, I'll be fine. I now have two escorts to take me safely to my uncle's."

"It's not too late to stay, Danielle," Sister Gertrude said, her face still worried.

"I belong with my uncle."

"Then, *enfant,* go with God and have a safe journey." Sister Gertrude kissed Danielle on both cheeks.

As Danielle started to step away, Gaby hugged her again, whispering in her ear, "Are you sure you'll be safe with that one?" Her gaze slid to Claude standing by two horses. "He looks so fierce."

"Yes." Danielle had learned long ago that looks were deceiving. The Marquis was a very handsome man who was as evil as the devil himself.

"Then it is good-bye, Danielle. I will miss you."

"And I you. I've never had a friend like you, Gaby. You must marry your Monsieur David, if that's what you want."

Gaby's laugh was shaky with suppressed tears. "Ah, most definitely. Godspeed."

Danielle hurried toward Monsieur Renoir, wiping at the tears that streaked her face. The Marquis had never allowed her to befriend other girls. Until her friendship with Gaby, Danielle hadn't known just how much she had missed. Her childhood had been an isolated one, with only stolen moments from time to time with Pierre, often with Margot in the middle.

Claude helped her to mount a chestnut mare, apologizing that the horse didn't have a sidesaddle. Danielle knew this would be one of many concessions she would have to endure on the journey. She waved away his concern and dismissed from her mind the unladylike way her gown rode up her legs. She dared not look back at Sister Gertrude as she spurred her horse forward to follow Monsieur Renoir.

Danielle focused her attention on the man astride a huge black stallion ahead of them. As Rouen urged his stallion toward them, horse and rider seemed as one, large and powerfully muscled. The early morning chill penetrated her cloak, causing her to shiver as her brown gaze locked with the dark gray of Rouen's. His look rendered her motionless astride her horse as though the world had faded away, leaving them alone with only primitive, animalistic urges to guide them.

When he pulled up along side of her, he blanked his expression, diffusing the charged intensity between them. "Good morning, Mademoiselle de Bussy," he said in a formal voice.

She nodded her greeting, fearing her voice would fail her.

"If at any time you tire, tell me. We will stop. Your uncle's cabin is usually a four-day trip."

She stiffened at his arrogant tone. "And so it shall be this time. I'm an accomplished rider, Monsieur. I'll not tire."

"I didn't realize riding was taught at a convent."

"I didn't always live in a convent," Danielle replied, then kicked her mare to go faster out of the unfinished fort.

Danielle stared at Rouen's strong, broad back, as she had for the past four days. She purposely erased the man in front of her from her mind and thought about Pierre's light brown hair and hazel eyes. She was so homesick for France and Pierre.

Every time she heard an unusual sound she jumped. Every time she saw something strange she tensed. She didn't belong here. For the first whole day she had pictured an Indian behind every tree. Her nerves were raw and frazzled. For the thousandth time, she wished she was home in France where she knew what to expect, where she knew the rules she must live by.

Here, in the Louisiana Colony, everything was foreign to her, especially Rouen Beauvoir. He was distant but polite to her, saying very little that wasn't necessary. Most of her conversations were with Claude, whom she had come to like and respect for his knowledge of this land. Claude had made the trip bearable, breaking the long silences with his observations of the country around them. Earlier in the day, she had seen a brown bear in the forest and had come to appreciate its beauty. Claude was teaching her the different bird calls, and she was beginning to distinguish them. She particularly liked the cardinal and the blue jay, splashes of bright color against a background of greens and browns.

An animal cry rang out in the pine forest, jerking her thoughts to the present.

" 'Twas only a mountain lion, Danielle. Nothing to worry about," Claude said as he brought his horse up close behind hers.

"Nothing! Didn't you tell me they were *big* cats?"

"He's too far away."

"How can you tell?"

"By the sound of his cry." When the trail widened, Claude rode alongside Danielle.

She was amazed at Claude's ability to tell the animals' footprints and how long they had been there. One time he had explained, after observing some tracks, that the fox had been injured because he was favoring one leg.

"How long have you lived here, Claude?"

"Came over in 1699 with Bienville's brother."

Danielle glanced over at her friend. "You've never missed France?"

"No. I have freedom here. Too many rules there."

"There are rules here, too. They differ from those in France."

A wide grin split his weathered face. "I guess you're right. I prefer nature's rules to man's."

Danielle stared again at Rouen's back. He lengthened the distance between them and disappeared around a bend in the trail. "How long have you known Monsieur Beauvoir?"

"I saved his life four years ago."

"What happened?" Danielle asked, hating the fascination with Rouen that led her to ask.

"Rouen hadn't been in the colony more than a month and everything was new to him. He stumbled onto a small band of Chickasaws who thought he would be good for an afternoon of sport. I persuaded them otherwise."

"Is that how you got your scar?"

"I received this"—Claude ran his finger along the red line—"when Rouen and I were hunting bison and he saved me."

"From Indians?"

"No, from a trapper who didn't like us hunting in his territory."

Fear rustled through Danielle like wind through the trees. Everything in the New World was so harsh. Violence was everywhere.

Suddenly Claude whipped around, drawing his knife in the same instant. Danielle froze, her fingernails stabbing into the palms of her hands, her throat tight with anxiety.

"Good evening," Rouen said, his look belying his polite greeting as he reined in his horse behind them. "Claude, if I had been an Indian, you wouldn't have had the time to pull out your knife. Leave the chitchat for another time."

"What's wrong with our talking to break the boredom?" Danielle bristled at the little trick Rouen had played on them. Her heartbeat had tripled its normal rate, and her breath came in shallow gasps.

"Things are too quiet. I don't like it."

"Too quiet? Are you not happy you hear no one?" Danielle was puzzled by Rouen's statement. Everything having to do with the New World—with him—puzzled her.

"I become most concerned when I don't hear anything. Indians never make their presence known until it's too late."

Her knuckles white as she gripped her reins, Danielle scanned the tall pine trees that dominated the landscape. Tension tightened the muscles in her neck and shoulders. Freeing one hand from her reins, she touched her blonde hair, covered with a straw hat that Sister Gertrude had given her to protect her from the harsh sun. All she could think of were the stories she had heard about Indians taking a person's scalp for their prize. Her head tingled with that thought, and a shudder passed through her body.

"Are they watching us right now?" Her voice quavered as she continued to search the area, sure that at any moment Indians would pounce on them.

"Possibly." Rouen's stern features relaxed into a half smile. "Danielle, if some Indians are watching us right now, they might be friendly ones. Not all of them are our enemies."

"Then why are they hiding?"

Rouen shrugged. "Perhaps they have no reason

to reveal themselves." He directed his horse around Claude and Danielle. "We'll make camp up ahead near the stream."

Her mouth fell open for a few seconds before she clamped it shut, her teeth meshing together. He expected her gladly to make camp when Indians could be lurking nearby ready to attack. Shouldn't they do something to defend themselves?

"Monsieur Beauvoir!" she called to his back, still using his formal name even though she had given up calling Claude Monsieur Renoir on the first hour of the journey.

Rouen glanced over his shoulder but said nothing.

Danielle prodded her mare forward until she was almost abreast of Rouen. "How much farther is it to my uncle's?"

"Two, possibly three more hours."

"Would it not be better to keep going and arrive there tonight?"

"No," was his clipped answer.

"But why not?"

"How long have you lived in the colony, *mademoiselle?*"

"Almost a week."

"And in that time you have become an expert on the forest?"

At his rebuke, Danielle sat up straight in her saddle. "I do think it would be safer in a cabin rather than out in the open by a campfire with no telling who is watching."

"You're right about a campfire. We won't make one tonight. But the woods are difficult to travel through when it's pitch black. You might stumble into something you don't want to," Rouen explained in an infuriatingly patient voice that caused Danielle to bristle even more.

"I do recall Claude telling me about how you stumbled into a band of unfriendly Indians shortly after your arrival in the colony, Monsieur Beauvoir," she said. She gritted her teeth, her gaze challenging him to disprove her.

He nodded, saying in a voice full of amusement, "My point exactly. Now, Mademoiselle de Bussy, if you'll permit us, we'll head for the camp area."

His emphasis on her name made it clear he thought the formality she was insisting on under the circumstances was ridiculous. "Certainly, Monsieur Beauvoir," she said. Inside, she fumed.

As she pulled her mare in between Rouen's and Claude's horses, thoughts tumbled through her mind. She wanted to show Rouen that she was perfectly capable of taking care of herself and didn't need him at all. She knew that was ridiculous, though. She felt like a fish out of water. Would she make it to her uncle's alive? She hated the fact that the Marquis might win in the end. At least he would never know that her long blonde hair had become some warrior's trophy.

Dismounting at the campsite, Danielle had to grip the mare for support. Her legs felt like churned butter. After four grueling days, she still wasn't used to riding long hours. But she would never tell Rouen. When she felt her legs steady, she let go of her mare and removed the saddle, painfully aware of her sore buttocks and thighs.

She couldn't help the slight limp to her walk as she led her mare to the stream for some water. Glancing over her shoulder, she caught Rouen staring at her with a devilish glint in his eyes. Of course he knew about every ache in her body. There was no way she could disguise her discomfort from a man who was so observant.

She looked back around and tried to ignore the pinpricks that rose along her spine as her mare drank the cool water. But she heard him approach, each footstep making her heart quicken. His scent was an aphrodisiac. Her tattered nerves screamed with weariness—and with anticipation.

Rouen paused next to Danielle while his stallion bent to drink. The air was charged with tension, subtle sparks springing to life between them. He had thought this trip would wash her from his mind. He wanted to ignore the attraction between them, but he found it impossible to forget her presence for one moment. She was a woman used to the comforts of a civilized world, but she had silently endured the pain and hardships of the past four days.

With each mile from Fort Louis, his admiration for her had grown. He was glad that tomorrow they would reach her uncle's. It would be difficult to forget Danielle, but it was best that he put as much distance between them as possible after he delivered her to Robert Havel. He and Danielle clashed like the colony's Indians.

"Without a fire, what will we eat?" Danielle asked in an attempt to ease the disquieting tension between them. Rouen seemed so comfortable with silence. She never had been, and during this journey she'd had more than her share of silence.

"Dried venison and some stale bread."

She stifled the moan that threatened to escape her lips. They had eaten the dried deer meat for every meal, but at least before with a fire they had a warm corn mash and beans. A vision of the apple torte the chef at the chateau often prepared for dessert tantalized her, as if its scent wafted through the forest. She ran her tongue over her lips, savoring in her mind the sweet delicacy. At the moment, she would give anything to have one bite.

"The thing I hate the most about these trips is the food. I miss Marte's cooking."

"Marte's?" There was a breathless quality to her voice as Danielle turned slightly toward him, her pulse racing involuntarily at the mention of another woman.

"Marte is my housekeeper. I was lucky to find her at the fort. Not knowing how to cook or clean made life here in the colony less than desirable."

Is Marte unmarried? How old is she? Is she beautiful? Why do I care? "How long has she worked for you?"

"Two years. Her husband died on the boat coming to the colony."

Her gaze shifted to the water flowing swiftly downstream, but she could still feel his gaze on her. Her skin pricked with heated awareness at each place it touched. "Before I left the fort, Sister Gertrude took great pains to lecture me about the shortage of women in the colony and about my duty as one of the few. Why hasn't Marte remarried?"

Rouen chuckled, a deliciously sexy sound. "She told me in a no-nonsense voice that thirty years married to one man was enough. I think she likes her independence." He winked at Danielle, as if to say he knew why she was probing, then took the reins of his stallion and led him away from the water.

Her cheeks reddened, and she stamped her foot

on the muddy bank, nearly losing her balance and slipping into the cold water. She didn't care what he thought! He could have all the Martes in this world and it would mean nothing to her. Absolutely nothing, Danielle thought fervently, as she guided her mare from the stream.

It was bad enough that they had to eat cold food, but when Danielle settled down to sleep, she nearly froze without the warmth of the fire they had enjoyed the previous nights. Curling up on her thin wool blanket, her cloak covering her, she tried to clear her mind. Her thoughts were inundated with images of Rouen winking roguishly at her, laughing huskily into her ear, staring intently at her from across the small space that separated them.

Pierre. She must concentrate on him and the wonderful times they had spent together as they had grown up. She vividly remembered once riding with total abandon across a field, Pierre racing her to the fence, letting her think she was winning until near the end. She had glanced over and seen—Rouen!

Damn! Double damn! Danielle pounded her fist into the earth and rolled over, trying to find a comfortable position. Every muscle ached and the ground was rock hard, the pebbles biting into her flesh. Tomorrow she would be free of Rouen and the strange spell he cast. Tomorrow she would be with family again and have a home. Tomorrow she would begin planning her revenge against the Marquis with Uncle Robert. Tomorrow would be the start of a new life. She finally drifted into a fitful sleep.

The next morning, Rouen gave Danielle less than fifteen minutes to get ready to ride. She quickly ate some dried meat, washed her face at the stream, and mounted her mare, feeling drained from the lack of sleep and her turbulent thoughts.

As she fell in behind Rouen, she called out to him, "Why do you hurry so this morning?"

"I have an itch." He answered her without looking back.

"An itch?"

Rouen didn't answer her question. He had already set his horse into a canter. Claude replied, "Whenever Rouen feels there's trouble brewing, he gets this itch." Claude shrugged. "I've learned not to question it. It saved my life once."

For the next three hours, Danielle was alert for the trouble that Rouen felt was near. But everything was quiet and peaceful. She began to think there was nothing to his itch until they crested the hill that overlooked her uncle's farm. Dark gray smoke billowed upward into the sky, fouling the air. There was an unearthly silence in the valley below.

FIVE

"Dismount." Rouen's clipped whisper sent a shaft of fear down Danielle's spine.

She did as he commanded, her gaze glued to the smoke that billowed over the clearing below like a menacing fog, making it difficult to see anything. Her heartbeat slowed to a painful throb, its pressure expanding in her chest. Somehow she knew her uncle's cabin was burning.

"We'll approach on foot," Rouen ordered in the same chilling whisper. He tied his stallion to a branch.

Danielle again followed his orders, her hands shaking so badly it took several minutes to tie her reins to a tree. While she struggled with the leather straps, she heard Claude and Rouen discussing her in whispers. Finishing her task, she walked determinedly toward them. Both men stopped talking and stared at her.

"I won't be left behind," she declared after a full minute had passed and no one had said anything.

"Claude will stay with you. I'm going to scout the situation out."

"No!" Fear raised her voice to panic level.

Rouen's hand shot out to cover her mouth. "Shh!

For heaven sakes, Danielle, be quiet!" The hiss of his voice underscored the seriousness of the situation.

Trembling, she nodded her understanding, and Rouen removed his hand. Drawing in the smoke-saturated air, she tried to calm her rapid heartbeat, but its pounding thundered in her ears. Sweat beaded her forehead, her panic and fear chasing away the cold.

"We go together. I won't remain behind. Me, I must know what has happened to my uncle. I'm not easily shocked," she added bravely, even though she was scared to death and overwhelmed with all that had happened to her in the past months. She did feel safer, though, with both men. She couldn't sit and wait for Rouen to return—or worse, not to return.

His gaze clashed with hers for a tension-fraught moment. Without a word, Rouen walked away to stare down at the burning cabin. He spoke with his back to her. "I know what we will find. Shock does not describe it. But, Danielle, I won't deny you the chance to discover what has happened to your uncle and his family." He slowly turned to face her, his eyes a soft gray like the pearl-colored dawn. "I imagine it's safe now."

Mesmerized by the compassion on his face, Danielle swallowed hard, trying to banish the uneasy flutter in her throat that his look produced. In all this primitive territory, only he made her feel safe, protected, something she hadn't truly experienced since she had been a child and her father had been alive. She had stood alone—until now.

For a brief moment, they were connected as

though they had known each other all their lives. A quick smile gentled the harsh planes of his face before the poignancy of the moment shattered when he started down the hill. She watched him descend, transfixed by the graceful power of his movements.

"Danielle?" Claude gently whispered, touching the small of her back to urge her forward.

Amazed that she could become so wrapped up in Rouen that she forgot where she was, Danielle fell into step behind him. He withdrew his long knife from its sheath at his waist. She didn't want to think of what had just transpired between them and what might transpire down below in the valley. Instead, she focused all her attention on the shiny metal of the knife and erased all thoughts from her mind except putting one foot in front of the other as she descended the hill.

Rouen halted at the edge of the clearing surrounding her uncle's cabin. When Danielle came up beside Rouen, thoughts and sensations began to filter through her mind again: the stench of burning wood, the sting of the smoke-laden air, the oppressive pressure in her chest threatening her next breath, the sight of several arrows sticking out of the ground.

She quickly scanned the destruction for her uncle. Hope blossomed in her heart when she couldn't find him.

"I would guess this happened about two hours ago," Rouen said. Claude nodded agreement.

"Uncle Robert might still be alive. He isn't here." Danielle gestured toward the burnt cabin, striving to detach herself from the scene.

"It's a possibility," Rouen replied almost absently

as he again carefully inspected the area to make sure no one was around. They stepped into the clearing.

Moving cautiously toward the cabin, Rouen was vigilant, not allowing himself to be lulled into a sense of safety. There had been times before when the Indian raiders had returned. He was acutely conscious of Danielle right behind him. He felt a deep sense of responsibility toward her.

Rouen knew the dangers of the wilderness, especially lately with the increased raids by the Chickasaws against the French settlers. He shouldn't have agreed to escort her to her uncle's. At least at the fort she had been safe. But knowing her as he was beginning to, she would have found a way to travel to her uncle's with or without him. She was a determined woman with more stubbornness than was good for her.

A movement out of the corner of his eye brought Rouen spinning about with his knife raised, his body tense. A chicken scurried across the yard, and a laugh of relief rumbled from his chest. His determination to let nothing happen to Danielle stretched his watchfulness until he felt he would snap with the slightest provocation. When had her safety become so important to him?

He glanced toward Danielle and watched her search the area for any sign of her uncle. He knew what they would find eventually, and he wished he could protect her from what she would see—from what she would feel.

Oblivious to the chicken racing away, Danielle stared at the burnt hulk of the cabin. She separated from Claude and Rouen and walked toward it. The cabin was a smoldering mass of gray ashes. Only the stone chimney remained standing.

It was too hot to step inside what had once been her uncle's home, but Danielle felt compelled to examine it for the charred remains of him or his family. Heat swirled about her as her gaze ran over every inch of the cabin once, then twice.

Wiping the sweat from her brow with the back of her hand, she relaxed her shoulders slightly and swung around to face Rouen, who was bent down examining one of the arrows. "No one was in the cabin." She knew her hope was evident in her face and voice. "Perhaps my uncle was away when the Indians raided his farm."

Rouen's gaze fused with hers. Within his gray eyes, Danielle saw skepticism. Her hope began to die, replaced by fear for her uncle and his family, fear for Rouen, Claude, and herself.

Claude knelt down beside Rouen and whispered something, pointing toward the field behind the burnt cabin. Danielle followed the line of his outstretched arm but didn't see anything.

Rouen stood. "Danielle, Claude has found your uncle. He—"

Danielle suddenly knew what was out in the field, hidden from her view. Without thinking, she began to run toward the area where Claude had pointed. She heard Rouen shouting at her, but her legs wouldn't stop, her gaze intent upon the place in the field where her uncle lay. She raced toward the only link to a happy past when her father had been alive and her uncle had often visited them, playing with her, laughing with her.

The pounding in her temples matched the pounding of her feet against the dirt, drowning out all other sounds. As she rounded the side of the cabin, Rouen caught up with her, grasping her about the waist and bringing her back flat against his chest. The sudden impact of her body against his knocked the breath from her. She gulped for air as his arms locked about her, imprisoning her before she could wiggle free. She hammered her fists into his arms while her foot kicked back against his shin. He cursed, but his hold remained tight.

"Let me go!" she cried out in frustration and anger.

"No!" he replied, equally angry.

"You're a—" She was so enraged at Rouen she couldn't even finish her sentence. Instead, she renewed her efforts to free herself, trying to pry his arms from her front, her fingernails digging into his hard flesh and drawing blood.

"What am I, *ma petite?*"

His embrace strengthened about her until she thought he would squeeze the last breath from her lungs and she would faint. *"Cochon!* Pig! Bully! Brute!" The words came in gasps as she tried to inhale the smoke-drenched air.

"Ah, a woman who appreciates my finer attributes."

The teasing edge to his words siphoned the fight out of her. As quickly as she began to run, she went still in his arms, her body limp, her head sagging forward as if in defeat. "Please, Rouen."

His heart wrenched at the anguish in her voice, but he kept his arms about her. He could feel her racing heartbeat, her panting gasps as she tried to calm herself. He took a deep breath laced with her clean scent. It warred with the smells of death. No woman should have to deal with what he knew was out in the field.

When her heartbeat slowed and her breathing eased, he gently turned her within his embrace so he could look at her. He placed his thumb under her chin and tilted up her face. Her eyes shone with unshed tears. In that moment, he wanted to protect her from any further hurt more than anything else. In that moment, he never wanted to be the cause of her pain.

"Listen, Danielle," he implored, waiting to make sure she was listening. "Claude is taking care of your uncle. It isn't a pretty sight."

"I should be the one to bury him."

He captured her face between his large hands, his look softening. "No, *ma petite.*"

"I'm his family, not Claude."

The hysterical ring to her words alarmed Rouen. When she tried to break free, his hands slipped down to her shoulders, and he shook her. She went still, but the trapped look in her eyes tore at his heart.

"Danielle, you can't. Please understand."

"But why?"

Rouen's jaw clenched. He didn't want to have to tell her.

"Why?" she repeated, her dark brown eyes puzzled.

"They tortured him."

She tensed, her eyes dilated, all color drained from her face. "Why? What did my uncle do to them?"

Rouen swore softly and drew her against him, his

arms about her like a shield of comfort. Cushioning her cheek against his shoulder, he wished he could absorb her anguish into himself. "Those questions can't be answered simply. Some Indians don't want the French here because their tribe is allied with the English. It's their way of fighting their enemy, and the French are their enemy."

"So because my uncle was French, he was murdered." She leaned back to stare up into his face.

"Men have killed for far less than that."

"Violence seems to be a way of life for men." A hardness entered into her voice as she straightened, rejecting the solace Rouen offered her. All she had seen in the colony had been death and destruction. "I'm fine now. You needn't worry about me."

Her emotionless voice and expression worried Rouen even more than before, but he didn't show it as he released her. Danielle watched quietly from a distance as Claude dug a grave for her uncle. Her bearing was proud, her stance erect.

When Claude finished, she calmly walked to the grave, knelt beside the freshly turned mound of dirt, and said a silent prayer. Rouen stood behind her with his head bent, concealing the concern etched into his features. All of sudden she had changed from an almost hysterical woman to a stoic one. He didn't like it. She was shutting off her emotions. What would happen when she was forced to face them, as he had painfully discovered would happen?

When Danielle rose a few minutes later, she rounded on Rouen. "Where's my uncle's wife?"

"I don't know. The Indians might have taken her prisoner."

"And my uncle's daughter?"

"The same. But Claude and I will look around to make sure before we leave."

"I'll help."

"I don't—"

"I won't be prevented from searching."

The strength in her resolve convinced Rouen to allow her to help. It would be useless to fight her on this. "As you wish."

Danielle began at the cabin and worked her way outward, covering one side. Rouen and Claude searched the other sides. She didn't permit herself to think about what she would do if she found her uncle's wife or daughter, but she couldn't have stood by and watched as Rouen and Claude sought the rest of her family. She had to keep busy.

At the edge of the woods, she hesitated. The tall pines cast dark shadows across the ground, sending a shiver through her. She took first one step, then another, into the forest, her mouth dry. Moistening her lips with the tip of her tongue, she went several yards farther into the grove of trees, glancing back every few seconds to keep her eye on the clearing.

A rustling sound drifted to her and Danielle froze, her breath bottled in her lungs as she imagined Indians hiding behind every tree. She couldn't turn around and run back toward Rouen or call out to him. Her body and mind were paralyzed with fear. Words locked inside her throat.

A cry penetrated her haze of fear. A child's cry? Danielle forced herself to take in deep breaths as she listened. This time when she heard the noise, she was sure it was a child crying. She hurried forward, forgetting that she might become lost. She concentrated on the direction of the sound, not on the branches tearing at her gown or scratching her arms as she ran, making her own trail through the forest.

Danielle nearly stumbled over the child, covered with pine needles and branches. A startled gasp escaped Danielle's lips as she halted, knelt beside the tree, and frantically tossed the debris off the sobbing child.

The little girl, who couldn't have been more than three years old, was tied to the tree. Tears streamed down her plump, red cheeks, and her dark brown eyes were huge with fright. The child's hair was brown, her skin dark. Danielle knew it was her cousin. There was a look about the eyes that reminded Danielle of her uncle.

Cooing softly to the hysterical child, Danielle quickly loosened the gag that had fallen about the child's neck, then the rope that held her to the tree. Her throat closed, and she had to swallow several times to keep herself from faltering. She could imagine the panic and horror that had gone through her uncle's head as he had forced himself to tie his only child to the tree in the hope his daughter wouldn't be found by the warriors raiding his homestead.

When she freed her cousin, Danielle drew the child into her arms, trying to convey her concern through her touch. "You'll be fine now. I won't let anyone hurt you." Her words came out in a raw whisper as she fought to keep her own emotions in control for her cousin's sake.

The child's sobs calmed as Danielle held her and talked in a singsong voice. Over and over, she smoothed the small girl's hair, picking out pine needles and twigs.

When Rouen came racing through the forest as fast as Danielle had, her cousin was asleep in her arms, her tears dried. Danielle glanced over her shoulder when Rouen nearly collided with them.

"Why in the devil are you sitting on the ground?" he stormed at her, relief and anger vying for supremacy in his expression.

She twisted around so Rouen could see the child in her lap. "I found her tied to the tree. My uncle must have hidden her here."

His anger fled from his expression. "I thought something had happened to you when I couldn't find you."

"Do you know my cousin's name?"

He lifted the small child from Danielle's lap. "It is Anne. We must leave. It grows late and I don't want to stay near here."

"Did you find Anne's mother?"

"Yes."

Danielle didn't need to ask if the woman was alive. His one-word answer said it all. His mouth was set in a grim, determined line, his strides lengthening as he made his way out of the forest. Danielle had to run to keep up with him.

As she followed Rouen across the clearing toward the cabin, she noticed Claude digging another grave alongside her uncle's. Though she hadn't known her uncle's wife, she felt a duty to say a prayer for her. As Danielle knelt beside the grave, she thought about the Indian woman who had married her uncle. Had she been murdered because she defied her culture and married a Frenchman? For an instant

Danielle wondered what would have happened to her and Pierre if they had dared defy the Marquis. Death? Chilled, she hugged her arms to her chest as she stood and walked toward Rouen and Claude.

Rouen carried the child as they climbed up the hill to the horses, but after Danielle mounted her mare, she said, "I want to hold Anne."

"She's sleeping. She'll be heavy," Rouen replied and started to turn away.

"She's *my* child now. I will hold her and care for her."

Rouen spun around, his gaze connecting with hers. His look pierced her proud countenance like an Indian arrow. "There's nothing wrong with accepting help, Danielle."

"I'm all Anne has now." *And she's all I have,* Danielle thought, feeling at the moment as if she would never see her homeland or her mother again. Quickly she dismissed the question of what she would do when she returned to Fort Louis. She had no answers and was afraid there wasn't an acceptable one. She didn't want to marry and become like her mother, at the mercy of a man for everything.

"As you please, *mademoiselle.*" Rouen lifted Anne up into the saddle in front of Danielle.

As he mounted his stallion, she adjusted Anne to fit in the curve of her arm. Somehow she would provide for them. She owed it to her uncle for the memories that had furnished solace on her long journey to this place.

There were several hours left in the day, and Rouen put as much distance as possible between them and her uncle's. As Danielle rode, she tried to think of a way to find food and shelter for herself and her cousin. She had four days to come up with a solution. Her dilemma helped divert her attention from the ache in her arm where she held Anne, but as the sun crept lower in the sky, Danielle could no longer ignore the muscles that protested her cousin's weight.

When they stopped for the night, Rouen took Anne from Danielle. Pinpricks of pain knifed up her arm, but she refused to tell Rouen.

When she dismounted, she said, "I will take care of Anne." She held her arms open for the child, schooling her look into one of fierce resolve.

After he thrust Anne into her embrace, Rouen walked toward Claude to help set up camp, muttering something under his breath. Danielle turned her full attention to Anne, who was awakening in her arms. She smiled down at her cousin as the little girl opened her eyes and looked up into Danielle's face, bewildered.

"Hello, Anne. I'm your cousin, Danielle. Your *papa* was my uncle."

Anne's tiny brow wrinkled. *"Papa,"* she said and looked around. *"Papa? Maman?"*

"They're gone, Anne. I will care for you from now on." Danielle sat down, cradling Anne in her lap as she combed her fingers through the child's tangled long hair. It still held traces of pine needles and twigs.

"I want *Maman, Papa."* Tears welled in Anne's eyes and fell onto her plump cheeks.

"I know, *ma cherie.* They had to leave, but they wanted me to love you like they did." Danielle wiped the tears from the child's face with the edge of her gown.

Danielle felt unprepared to handle the situation, at a loss as to what to do next. Her heart was heavy as she held Anne and rocked her back and forth, trying to soothe her with reassurances that Danielle had no idea how to keep. She didn't have a place to live or a means to provide food or clothing for herself, let alone Anne.

Danielle wanted to cry, too. She wanted to lean on someone, but she didn't dare let down her guard because she had Anne to take care of. It was a new feeling for Danielle to be needed. She had always needed Pierre's protection; she had needed her mother's love. Now it was her turn to give. That scared her.

SIX

Rouen watched Danielle place Anne on the bed of pine needles. The moonlight bathed Danielle's face in silvery radiance, but her delicately boned features were weary. Several times he had wanted to offer his help, but her proud expression earlier stopped him from making a fool of himself. She didn't want his help. It was that simple, and yet Rouen couldn't dismiss the picture of Danielle struggling to hold Anne in the saddle in front of her. He had known her arm hurt, but he also had known she would never admit she needed his help. She was determined to do everything alone, as though it were important to her that she need no one.

As he followed her with his gaze, he gritted his teeth until pain streaked down his neck. She gently covered the child with a blanket, whispering a few more soothing words even though Anne slept. Danielle's fingers remained on the girl, a caressing touch on the cheek. She would be a good mother. A vision of her holding his child in her arms, singing to their baby, took him by surprise.

His groin tightened as he looked at Danielle and wished it was him she touched. Damn, he wanted her. It had nothing to do with being the mother of his children. What he felt was pure lust, that was all. Yet that was enough to make him want to forget his promise to her about not letting anything happen that she didn't want.

She stood and stretched her cramped muscles, rolling her shoulders to ease the stiffness from them. Claude was already asleep a few yards away. When her gaze shifted and connected with Rouen's, her throat went dry and her breath caught. The scorching look he gave her burned through the winter night, making her uncomfortably warm.

"How's Anne?" Rouen asked, his voice rough. He sat on his haunches, absently drawing circles in the dirt with a stick.

"Confused. Exhausted. Scared." Danielle sat on a log near him, too tense to sleep, too tired to do anything else.

The silence stretched between them. Rouen drew his circle over and over while Danielle watched the repetitious movement, wishing somehow she could block all thoughts from her mind. She didn't want to think about her problems anymore. She had tried to come up with a solution earlier as they had traveled. She hadn't. Now her distress was beginning to take hold.

"What shall you do?"

"I don't know. I'm too tired to sleep." She shrugged, deliberately misreading him.

She wasn't ready to discuss her future with anyone, especially Rouen. Her uncle had been her only hope against the Marquis. Now she had Anne to consider. If her stepfather found her and made her return to France, he would never let Anne come, too. The child would be abandoned with no hope for a future. She couldn't allow that to happen.

As before, Rouen let the silence lengthen between them. The soft whistle of the wind through the forest, the sound of birds singing, suffused the night. He resumed making circles in the dirt. Why he wanted her to face her problems he didn't know, but he couldn't let it rest.

"Danielle, what will you do when we reach the fort?" He worded his question so she couldn't continue to avoid it.

Her head snapped up, her gaze clashing with his. In that moment, she sensed his ruthlessness and single-mindedness and realized she could no longer run. "I have no plan."

"We'll reach the fort in four days." Rouen dropped the stick and surged to his feet in one effortless motion.

Though his face was in the shadows, she knew he was staring intently at her. She felt it deep within, the earlier warmth turning molten. Her thoughts no longer revolved around her dilemma. Her mind centered on him, drawn to the quiet strength that mingled with a primal instinct for survival. He drained her emotionally. He would demand so much of her.

"I am aware of that." Her words came out stilted and weary. "I shall craft a plan before we reach the fort. I have had little time to think." She pushed herself off the log and rose unsteadily to her feet, her legs threatening to buckle beneath her. "Excuse me, *s'il vous plait.* I need some sleep. Tomorrow will be another long day."

But before she could walk to her blanket, his quiet

promise tingled down her spine. "Sleep for now, Danielle, but we'll talk later."

"Anne is *my* burden. Mine alone." She hated the desperate ring to her words, but she doubted she could spar verbally with him any longer.

"I promised Governor Bienville and Sister Gertrude that I would take care of you. I bear responsibility for you both."

"When did you speak to them?" Anger nibbled at what composure she had left. She didn't want others discussing her life, deciding her future. Only she would do that.

"The evening before we left."

"Sister Gertrude said naught of it to me."

"I asked her not to."

"Why?"

"Why should she?"

"Because you were discussing me."

"Actually, Danielle, we were discussing me. My intentions toward you."

"Which are?"

"My intentions were to deliver you safely to your uncle, nothing more."

"Then your responsibility is over. You delivered me safely."

"Not to your uncle, Danielle." Rouen moved closer. Moonlight highlighted the powerful lines of his body, the strong angles of his face.

He could protect her and care for her. She was so tired. It was tempting to let him take the reins, but she wouldn't follow the path her mother trod. After her husband died, her mother married the first man who asked. For the past ten years, she had lived in misery. She would never turn over her life to another.

Danielle held up her hand to ward him off. "Don't. I can take care of myself. I am responsible for myself." She had learned in the past months she was the only one she could trust. Even Pierre had violated the trust she had placed in him.

"True. But I can't help my feelings, either. I do feel responsible for your—safety, which at the moment is in question."

"From whom? You?"

His low chuckle was a delicious sound in the darkness of the night, sharpening the fine-honed tension gripping her. "Possibly. But I was thinking more about your future than this immediate moment."

This time when he stepped closer, Danielle didn't have the strength to raise her arm. His body was a breath away, and she felt overwhelmed by him, the scents of leather and the outdoors spinning a web around her as if to hold her his prisoner.

With his thumb, Rouen lifted her face until she was staring into his eyes. She felt lost in that instant, as though he had stolen away her will. She wanted to hate him for making her feel vulnerable and weak, but could think only of what his lips felt like when he kissed her. She wanted to feel them against hers again. She needed to feel safe, if only for a few minutes. She needed to feel alive.

He bent his head toward hers with excruciating slowness, his lips grazing hers in an infinitely gentle touch, then another, giving her time to respond or push him away. She wanted him to deepen the kiss. Her hands came up to frame his face and bring his mouth down harder upon hers, but he pulled back a few inches. Her fingers still pressed against his jaw. Before she could move them, he covered her hands with his. His strong, sensual gaze tethered hers, and her heartbeat went out of control, so violent and rapid that it dizzied her.

When his mouth settled over hers, she felt as though she were soaring above the earth. His tongue pushed its way inside; his hands traveled downward to cup her breasts where they strained against her gown. She ached for him, the heat singeing her frayed nerves. She wanted more, much more.

She thrust her tongue against his, dueling, parrying as though they were two fencers. Seeking entry into his mouth, she boldly swept through his defenses and tasted of him. Something inside of her shifted. She felt things she had never felt before and was momentarily confused by the intense sensations that pushed every thought aside but the man before her.

He nibbled a path to her earlobe and whispered, "I can set you up. See to your welfare, Danielle."

His proposition was like a cold slap in the face, and she stiffened. "Set me up?" The sensual haze lifted from her brain; icy reality struck. "What, as your mistress?" She wrenched herself from his embrace and put several feet between them, her chest rising and falling rapidly.

"I want to care for you and Anne." Anger roughened his voice to a growl.

She scrubbed at her mouth as though the feel of his had disgusted her. "I will be no man's mistress." Spinning about on her heel, she hurried to her blanket, her throat tight with emotions she had never wished to feel.

As she curled up to try and sleep, all she could

think about was Bridget and the humiliation her mother had suffered with that woman living in the chateau. Was the way she had returned his kiss the reason he thought she would become his whore? Did Bridget feel that way when she was with the Marquis? *Mon Dieu,* Danielle hoped not.

Fifteen minutes later her heart still beat fast. Her mind was filled with thoughts of herself and Rouen entwined in a lover's embrace. Mistress! His proposal made her fume. She would never be like Bridget. There had to be another way to care for herself and Anne besides selling her body.

When sleep came later, Danielle was whisked away into a world of dreams. She was in a sun-drenched meadow, dancing about in a field of flowers, their sweet fragrance wafting to her. Across the meadow Pierre waited for her, his arms outstretched. She ran to him, seeking the shelter of his embrace. She was only a few feet away when suddenly Rouen stood in the sunlight, his feet braced apart, his hands on his hips, waiting for her as though it were only a matter of time before she succumbed to his charms. The arrogant tilt to his head, the smug look on his face, attested to his self-assurance.

Danielle wanted to flee, but she couldn't. His sexuality hypnotized her, drawing her close.

She melted into his embrace, relishing his strong arms about her. His silky strokes along the length of her spine dissolved her last resistance. With her eyes closed, she leaned back to allow him free access to her neck. His tiny kisses seared a path along her neck to her ear. As he lovingly bit into the soft flesh of her lobe, Danielle wondered what it would be like to be truly loved by him.

As the question filtered through her bemused mind, teeth clamped down on her earlobe, sending a bolt of pain through her. The arms about her strengthened their hold until she thought she couldn't take another breath. Her eyes snapped open, and she stared into the Marquis's evil face. His hideous laughter bombarded her as he threw her to the flower-carpeted ground.

As suddenly as the Marquis appeared, he disappeared, replaced by an Indian, his face painted black and red, towering over her with a hatchet in his hand. He raised his arm. When it came down toward her head, Danielle shot up in her blanket, a silent scream trapped inside of her.

"Danielle?" Rouen was beside her, drawing her against him. "What's wrong?"

She quaked, seeking the warmth of his body, but the cold was entrenched deep inside of her. She couldn't stop her body from shaking. Though she opened her mouth to reply, no words formed.

"Did you have a nightmare?"

She nodded her head and burrowed deeper into the shelter of his arms. She was so frightened. She wanted to feel strong and sure, but she didn't.

"You're all right. I won't let anything happen to you. We'll get back to the fort safely."

His murmured reassurances calmed her. Somehow she believed him. She didn't want to depend on him or anybody else, but at the moment she had no choice. There would come a day when she wouldn't have to. There would come a day when she would be her own person, she vowed as she listened to the strong, comforting beat of his heart.

Minutes passed in silence. Rouen continued to

hold Danielle and she drew strength from his presence. He finally set her at arm's length.

"What do you run from, Danielle?"

She met his probing gaze with a serenity born from years of hiding her true, frightened feelings from her stepfather and his daughter. The time had come to take a risk. "I flee the Marquis Duchamp."

Rouen frowned, removing his hands from her. "The Marquis Duchamp? Why do you run from him?"

"Do you know him?"

"I know of him," he lied, not ready to reveal who he was to Danielle. He had met the Marquis several times at court. What he knew of the man was chilling. He was a tyrant who loved to control people, using cruel methods for his sadistic pleasure. "Why, Danielle?"

"He's my stepfather."

"And?" The cold of the night penetrated to the marrow of his bones. Images of Danielle at the mercy of the Marquis Duchamp crowded Rouen's mind.

"And he tried to . . . to have his way with me."

He fisted his hands, his anger a red-hot poker goring him. He gritted his teeth to control his fury. If he ever saw the man, he would . . .

"He wanted me to be his mistress."

Her words struck Rouen like the flat of a broadsword. He was no better than the Marquis Duchamp.

"I declined his offer by hitting him over the head with a candelabrum. If you know of the Marquis, you know he is not a forgiving man. I fled France because no one could protect me there. The only one I knew who would have stood up to my stepfather was Uncle Robert."

"How long has your mother been married to the Marquis?" Rouen asked. He knew of the man's reputation, but not much else. Rouen had avoided court life and the gossip surrounding it when he had lived in France.

"Ten years."

"The Marquis never tried to—make you his mistress before?"

Danielle leaped to her feet and towered over Rouen, her hands balled at her sides. "No! I am lucky, *non?* I lived ten years in fear of the Marquis's riding crop only." Sarcasm etched her voice and temper flared in her eyes, making them almost black. "For the devil's own reasons, the Marquis left me alone until after he betrothed his daughter to the man I was to marry. With Pierre's engagement no one would stand up for me."

Rouen rose slowly, his expression hidden in the darkness of night. "What of your mother?"

"She's powerless against him. Everyone is. Even Pierre couldn't stop the engagement between the two families. The Marquis holds Pierre's father's markers."

The hopelessness of her situation cloaked her like a well-worn cape. She turned away, her shoulders sagging, her head bent. Tears sprang to her eyes, but she fought against them. They would do her no good. She had learned that lesson long ago.

Rouen touched her shoulders, laying his hands upon them. The warmth of his fingers brought her head up. Blinking her tears away, she swung around, evading his touch.

"My uncle was the only one I knew who would protect me against the Marquis. Uncle Robert hated him. It was because of the Marquis that my uncle left France. My stepfather delights in destroying lives. One day I'll return the favor." Steel determination edged her voice as the tears evaporated like the mist in the morning.

"Perhaps we can help each other, Danielle."

"How?" she asked suspiciously, remembering his earlier proposal of becoming his mistress.

"I'm in need of a wife to satisfy my father."

"I can't—"

"Hear me out before you answer." Rouen walked a few paces from Danielle. "My father is the Duc de Beauvoir. Until recently, I was the second son and unimportant to the future of the Beauvoir estates. When my brother and nephew died in an accident, the responsibilities of the family became mine, according to my father. He arranged a marriage for me that ended with my wife's death in childbirth. Now he desires me to marry again. The bride has been chosen—my brother's wife, Liliane. I will not bow to my father a second time, not after living here in freedom."

"Your father is very powerful in France."

"Then you also know that marriage to me places you under my family's protection. The Marquis Duchamp dares not touch you as long as you're my wife."

"When do you return to France?"

"Within the year. I cannot yet give this up." He swept his arm wide to indicate the wilderness about them.

Danielle couldn't understand what Rouen saw in

the tall trees that surrounded them, enclosing them in an alien world she wanted no part of. Suddenly it seemed as if they were the only two people alive. She remembered his earlier kiss and became desperate to think of anything but them together in an intimate embrace. She asked the first thing that popped into her mind. "What will your father say about your marrying me?'

Rouen's laugh was short and derisive. "He'll be angry because I didn't do as he wished, but he must live with my choice. If a marriage is to be arranged, I shall do the arranging."

"Earlier you wanted me as your mistress. Now you want me as your wife?"

"I must marry. I have a duty to my family that I cannot forsake. Though I should love to defy my father, for the sake of peace in the family I must marry someone from a similar background to mine."

Her heart twisted at the cold, calculating way he had explained his decision. Marriages were arranged every day. This would be no different, except that she could choose her husband. "I don't love you." Her throat tightened about the words, making them husky, a shade unsteady.

"Nor I you. So you see, this is for the best. We will not hurt each other."

"Yes, of course." She heard herself talking about marriage and love to this man as though it were nothing, a casual thing. In reality, she was scared of what she would be committing herself to and scared of the feelings he provoked in her.

"Good. You'll be protected from the Marquis, Anne will have a home, and I'll be rid of my father's meddling. Love need not enter into our marriage. I've found love complicates people's lives."

Danielle chewed her bottom lip. She couldn't allow her hurt feelings to grow. She had to look at her problem as coldly as Rouen had. A marriage of convenience. What other solution did she have? Everything he said made sense.

If she were realistic with herself, her only other choice was to return to the fort and marry some colonist who planned to live in the territory forever. With Rouen, she could return to France as a future duchess. She could use the resources of the Beauvoir family to destroy the Marquis. She would never have to pretend to be someone she wasn't or to feel something she didn't feel. Rouen didn't want her love; she didn't want Rouen's love. It was for the best—she had no love to give. The solution was simple.

"I have one condition to add to this proposal," Danielle said.

Rouen chuckled, moving closer until he was only a foot away. "One of the things I like about you is your boldness. I offer the best answer to your problem and you want a condition."

Danielle stood her ground, even though she wanted to back away. His nearness always made her pulse quicken. Rouen was handsome, with an air of daring and relentlessness that was fascinating and even appealing. She dared not yield to his masculine charms.

"When we return to France, I wish to go to court."

"Why?"

"I have dreamed of going to Versailles. The Marquis wouldn't let me."

He expelled a deep sigh. "I abhorred court life, but we shall go for a while. It'll be expected of us."

"Then I accept." She held out her hand to shake on the deal.

Rouen looked down at her hand then back up at her face. He closed his fingers around hers and drew her flat against him. "I have a condition to add, too."

As his whisper washed over Danielle, her heart began to speed. "What?"

"From the very beginning, we will be husband and wife in every sense. I'm expected to produce an heir."

Her cheeks flamed as she dropped her gaze to his doeskin jacket. It was a duty she realized she had to perform, but that didn't mean she would like it. She remembered hearing her mother crying after the Marquis had roughly taken her in the library. Danielle had hidden behind the sofa. She hadn't seen anything, but the sounds would stay in her mind forever. The Marquis's taunts and grunts still sent tremors through her. Something that sounded so disgusting had to hurt and humiliate.

"Look at me, Danielle," Rouen gently demanded.

She raised her head. The moon's rays sculpted his face with strength and power. As his wife, she would be safe from her stepfather. Rouen commanded his own life to the point of defying his father. He would never allow the Marquis Duchamp to harm something that was his.

Was she trading one prison for another? No, she wouldn't let Rouen control her life as the Marquis had. She would be a good wife to Rouen in return for his protection and his family name, but he would have no part of her heart and soul.

"Do you understand, *ma petite?*"

"Yes," she murmured, wanting to deny him the endearment but realizing he would use it anyway.

"Good. I have wanted you from the moment I saw you at the jetty."

His declaration should have frightened her. Instead, she closed her eyes, waiting in sweet anticipation for his next move. When his mouth bore down upon hers, some invisible force stripped her of the will to resist. She was achingly aware of every corded muscle that pressed against her softness. When he drew her closer, as if trying to transfuse his body heat into her, her pulse went wild beneath his hands. The pressure of his mouth on hers conveyed his longing, and she responded by molding herself to his hard contours and parting her lips to accept the invasion of his tongue. It delved inside, sweeping the honeyed cavern with a challenge.

Again those intense, wild sensations swept through her as his tongue explored the inside of her mouth. She began to lose the essence of herself in him. To save her own life, she couldn't stop it from happening.

With a savage curse he tore his mouth from hers and put Danielle at arm's length. His breathing was ragged, his grip on her arms tight, almost painful. "We shall marry as soon as we return to the fort."

She needed time to harden herself against him. She needed time to get her fragile emotions under control. It had to be because of all she had gone through in the past several months. Normally she would never allow someone so close, so quickly. "Perhaps we should wait—"

He placed his fingers over her mouth. "Shh. I cannot wait, but this isn't the time to take what I want. You and Anne need a protector."

The possessive ring to his words reminded her of what she would be to him—a possession, a means to bear him the heir he needed. It erased the last remnants of her desire. "Please remove your hands. We aren't married yet."

His chuckle mocked her, but he released her. "For now, *ma petite.*"

Danielle thought of several apt names to call him, but since she had committed herself to becoming his wife, she decided for once to hold her tongue. Instead, she went to her blanket and lay next to Anne to try and sleep. She didn't think she would be able to, but the last thing she remembered was his soft laughter. Then it was morning and Rouen was gently waking her.

"We must be going."

She opened her eyes to meet his devouring gaze as he knelt beside her. His intent look produced a tight, aching dryness in her throat. "Anne?"

"Claude is seeing to her."

"But I should."

"You must eat this first. We have a long day ahead of us." He thrust a piece of dried venison into her hand and stood before she could protest.

Danielle looked around to find Claude who was making a game out of breakfast. Anne giggled and grabbed at the meat. Danielle relaxed and bit off a piece of her food. Watching Claude with Anne made

Danielle smile. For a few minutes, she forgot about her bargain with Rouen.

But soon Rouen demanded that they head out, and Danielle was instantly reminded that before the week was out he would be her husband. The realization made her hot and cold at the same time.

Mounting her mare, she waited for Rouen to give her Anne, but instead he handed the child to Claude. Angered at his high-handedness, she declared, "Anne rides with me."

"We'll take turns holding Anne." Rouen didn't wait for her response. He walked past her and climbed into his saddle.

She stared at his back, gripping her reins so tightly that her knuckles turned white. Short of dismounting and trying to wrestle Anne from Claude, Danielle was helpless; Rouen would have his way. His features were set in a resolve that equaled hers. She had met her match, she realized with a feeling of foreboding.

What if he turned out to be like the Marquis, who had been so charming and accommodating to her mother until they had married? The Marquis had fooled her mother. Instinctively Danielle rejected that idea. She had seen Rouen in a situation where civilization had been stripped away and where his essence was evident in the way he dealt with danger—straightforward and with a strength that amazed her.

They rode for several hours. Danielle asked when they were going to stop to rest for Anne's sake and to change who was holding the child. Rouen answered soon, then turned his attention back to the trail.

Danielle first realized something was wrong when

she saw Rouen tense. He pulled his horse to a stop and indicated Danielle and Claude do the same. Then she heard the noise that had aroused Rouen's suspicion. A scream exploded through the air, sending a shaft of terror through Danielle.

Rouen motioned for everyone to dismount. Quietly they crept toward an outcropping of rocks that overlooked a farm. Danielle went deathly pale at the sight below, instantly shielding Anne with her body.

SEVEN

Below, surrounding a cabin on fire, were twenty warriors, their faces painted different colors and designs, their hair shaved on the sides and standing straight up on top of their heads. They toyed savagely with a man, taking cruel pleasure in slicing him with their knives as the man's screams impaled the air.

Danielle felt sick to her stomach. Twisting away, with her hands cupped over Anne's ears, Danielle fought down the nausea. She tried to block the hideous sounds from her thoughts, but it was useless. The man's dying screams invaded her mind like a monstrous demon.

Withdrawing his own knife from its sheath, Rouen started to move away. Claude clamped his hand about Rouen's arm. "No. There's nothing anyone can do now," Claude whispered.

Rouen clenched his jaw and tried to contain his rage. He dared do nothing that would endanger Danielle and Anne. A wealth of feelings battled for dominance inside him, all centered on the helplessness he was experiencing while watching another man die. Finally resigned defeat won, and he nodded his head, vowing to discover the identity of the

Frenchman behind these raids and put a stop to his traitorous actions.

Mercifully the screams died as the man died. Danielle offered a silent prayer for the settler's soul and one for themselves. She knew instinctively to remain still and keep Anne quiet, or they would become the raiding party's next victims. Danielle held her cousin tight and rocked her, desperate to shield her from further hurt.

Danielle had never felt such fear in her life, not even when the Marquis had tried to rape her. Stark, brittle flashes of the scene below came unbidden into her thoughts, and it took all her strength to sit quietly and wait. She wanted to flee as fast and as far as her feet would carry her, but they would only survive this day if the Indian raiders didn't discover their presence.

"We need to see to the dead," Rouen said an eternity later, when the eerie silence had taunted them until she thought she would go mad.

Rouen faced Danielle. His thumb under her chin, he compelled her to look him in the eye. "Stay here with Anne. You'll be safe. The Chickasaws went in the opposite direction. If we're lucky, they have shed enough blood today and are returning home."

"And if they aren't?" The burning in her throat weakened her voice.

"Then another family will fall victim to the raiding party."

"Or us?"

He nodded, the pain and horror in his eyes mirroring the feelings churning inside of her. For a brief moment she wanted to reach out and comfort him. She wanted to make him forget what they had seen, to make herself forget what they had seen. She needed his arms about her, his promises that she would be all right, that they would make it safely back to the fort.

"Danielle, I don't want you or the child down there. Will you stay here?" Rouen whispered in a voice that was tired, as though the energy had been drained from him.

"Yes." She dared not defy him this time.

Claude and Rouen left the ridge and made their way down to the farm. Continuing to hold Anne and whisper soothing words as much for herself as for the child, Danielle glanced about her at the forest. The green pines mocked her presence in the territory; the breeze seemed to shout at her to leave before it was too late. She didn't belong here.

She hated this place more each day. Some people, like Rouen and Claude, might see beauty in this land and forest, but all she saw was death and ugliness. Never would she forget what she had seen this day; it would stay in her mind, a part of her forever. After she married Rouen, she would try to persuade him to leave the colony as soon as possible.

When Anne fell asleep, Danielle gently placed the child on a bed of pine needles and ventured a glance at Rouen and Claude below. They had finished digging a grave and were lifting a bloody mass of flesh into it.

Danielle felt dirty and sick again. She stumbled to her feet, frantically looking about her. Remembering they had passed a stream only a few yards back, she headed toward it, wishing she could submerge herself until she was cleansed of these feelings of hopeless grime.

Light-headed, she glanced back at Anne to make sure the child was still asleep before kneeling on the bank and cupping her hands into the water. Its iciness cooled her fevered cheeks, and her world quit spinning. Drawing in deep, fortifying breaths, Danielle closed her eyes and listened to the water rushing over the rocks.

I'll make it back to France. She repeated the words over and over in her mind. She wouldn't let her stepfather win with her death in the New World.

Suddenly Danielle was yanked upward and spun about to face Rouen. Angry lines slashed his features as his gaze cut her like a long knife.

"What in the hell are you doing? I have enough to worry about without having to watch you every second. When I told you to stay, I meant stay where I left you." Rouen's fingers dug into the flesh of her upper arms as he shook her.

Her own temper escalated. "I didn't ask you to worry about me. I'm not ten feet away from the ridge." She gestured toward the area, realizing as she did that the underbrush partially blocked the view of the stream. But she was beyond caring that he had a reason to be angry. Everything crashed in on her as she returned his glare with open defiance.

"Next time I tell you to stay some place, you'd better stay." He squeezed the words out through clenched teeth. "I don't need to worry about you wandering off and getting yourself killed." The full censure of his gaze lanced into her.

"I don't need a keeper. I will marry you for the

protection of your name, but that is all. I'll earn my way in this world, even as your wife."

"You're damned right you will, starting now." Rouen pulled her hard against him while his mouth ground into hers, the force of his kiss driving her head back. His body shifted and tightened along her length. His one hand fisted in her hair; the other slid down her back, molding her more firmly against him.

Her senses and body began to succumb to his assault. Her mind fought against it. She brought her booted foot down on his. Swearing, he shoved her away from him, and she nearly fell into the stream. Steadying herself, she confronted him, her fury evident in her expression.

"You'll never own me. I may have few choices concerning my future, but if you try that again, I shall not marry you." She dragged a shaky hand through her hair, trying to bring order to it as well as to her riotous nerves. She was more upset at herself than Rouen. She had almost given in to him.

The anger left his expression, the harsh planes of his face easing into a neutral facade. He had locked himself behind a barricade, his emotions protected. "Very well, *mademoiselle.* My manners have gone begging. I should behave like the gentlemen you're accustomed to."

The mocking tone of his words made her suspicious. She backed away, a wary expression on her face. His stance, so proud and aloof, was as untamed and fierce as the rugged forest about them. She must have been crazy to accept his proposal of marriage! The only way she saw any peace in her future was not to yield to his male power.

Rouen bowed, sweeping his arm across his body as expertly as any courtier at Versailles, and said in an extremely polite voice, "I leave you to your privacy, Mademoiselle de Bussy, but do not tarry. We must be on our way as soon as Claude scouts the area."

She watched him leave, her face still wary. Her fingers touched her soft, kiss-swollen lips. Closing her eyes, she tried to banish the rogue from her thoughts, but tantalizing, haunting memories of their recent encounters plagued her bemused mind. She couldn't allow him to exert the devastating, effortless domination he had these past few days. She had to fight it.

Quickly Danielle knelt again at the stream to cool her heated face and bring order to her traitorous senses. Splashing water on her cheeks, she relished its cold bite. Tilting back her head, she raised her face to the sun's rays that filtered through the trees. She wanted to forget everything for the few minutes left to her. She centered all her thoughts on the branches of the pines gently swaying in the wind. A cardinal landed on a branch, its blood-red color a vivid reminder of what she had witnessed in the past few days.

A faint sound broke her concentration. The bird took flight, and pinpricks rose on her flesh. She looked straight ahead to find a band of Indians with long black hair and tattoos on their skin staring at her. She tried to cry for help, but nothing came out. Her body was immobilized with terror. She remembered the man's dying screams, his body red with his own blood, and yet she couldn't move even to stand and try to run.

Then all of a sudden nothing mattered. A serenity that she had never experienced dissolved the fear, as though her mind and body had reached the limit of terror it could experience in twenty-four hours.

Danielle rose slowly, her gaze trained on the Indian who appeared to be the leader. He was dressed in a garment of feathers woven into cords that covered his torso. Animal-skin leggings were tucked into moccasins similar to Rouen's. She was prepared for death and would face it with as much dignity as possible. Saying nothing, she directed her intent gaze at the leader, a small gesture of bold recklessness.

A lifetime passed in the seconds she assessed him and he her.

A movement caught her attention out of the corner of her eye, and she swept her gaze toward the distraction. Another warrior came forward, carrying Anne in his arms. Not the child! She couldn't let anything happen to Anne. A new fear took hold as Danielle rushed toward the Indian holding her cousin.

"No! Don't touch her. She's only a baby."

Danielle made it to the warrior who had Anne, but before she could reach out for the child, another Indian grasped her from behind and lifted her off the ground, her feet dangling inches above the earth. She kicked; she fought with pounding fists, but to no avail. As before with Rouen, she wasn't strong enough to win against this warrior.

Cursing the fact she was a female, she muttered several unladylike words.

"*Mon ami,* your woman has spirit."

The leader's voice halted Danielle's struggles. She looked around to see to whom the Indian spoke in French. Rouen stood a few yards behind her, smiling, his eyes gleaming silver. Her cheeks flamed, her temples hammered with frustrated rage.

"What's wrong with you? Have you gone mad? They have Anne!" she shrieked at Rouen, hoping to make him understand the gravity of the situation, never taking the time to wonder why he was still alive and smiling, too.

"Danielle," Rouen began in the patient voice she hated, "if he releases you, will you promise not to attack and to listen to what I have to say?"

The only thing she could do was nod her head.

After the warrior let her go and stepped back, Rouen walked to her. "These Indians are friendly with the French. They're the Choctaws. Your uncle's wife came from their tribe."

"I have come for the child called Whispering Wind," the leader said, again speaking in French.

Danielle grabbed Rouen's arm, her hold tight, desperate. "They can't have her."

"Whispering Wind is this woman's kin. Falling Water's husband was her uncle. We're taking the child back to Fort Louis to raise her as our own daughter." Rouen laid his hand over Danielle's. "Whispering Wind is young. She needs a woman. You already have several daughters, Running Wolf. I have none."

"You've pledged yourself to one another?" Running Wolf asked, a frown creasing his brow, indecision in his dark eyes as he looked from Danielle to Rouen, then back to Danielle.

"We will when we return to the fort. Whispering Wind will be welcome in our home."

Danielle held her breath, waiting to hear what the Indian leader would do. She knew if he wanted the child there was little she or Rouen could do. There were twelve warriors and only three of them.

"There's trouble brewing in the land. These raids will not be the last. Can you protect Whispering Wind?" the leader finally asked.

"Can you? Fort Louis is strong and far from the Chickasaws' domain. Whispering Wind will be safe," Rouen answered with more confidence than he really felt.

Danielle started to tell Running Wolf that the child would be leaving the New World for France within the year, but Rouen silenced her with a quick look, as though he had read her thoughts and didn't want to reveal that to the Indian leader.

"You're a good man, *mon ami.* You will raise Whispering Wind as your own."

Danielle sagged against Rouen in relief. Again she pulled a quaking hand through her tangled hair, drawing attention to its startling color. The warrior nearest her reached toward her and she dared not move. She stood immobile next to Rouen, her body plastered against his as the Indian touched her hair as if to discern if it were indeed the liquid gold it appeared, cascading down her back in thick waves. When the Choctaw released her hair, she offered him a trembling smile, sensing that she was doing the right thing.

"She is brave. We have been observing her," Running Wolf said when the warrior stepped away. "She will be a good mother for Whispering Wind."

The leader's words made Danielle feel proud. She felt as though she had passed some kind of test and that even in Rouen's eyes she was elevated.

"Can you tell me anything about these raids we have seen?" Rouen asked as Claude joined the group by the stream.

"We tried to warn Falling Water and her husband, but we were too late. There is an Englishman who has been traveling sometimes with the Chickasaw raiding party."

Rouen slid a glance toward Claude. "Do you know the Englishman?" Rouen asked Running Wolf.

"No."

"Have you seen him before?"

"I haven't seen him. One of my warriors out hunting reported to me about the Englishman. There are also rumors that someone is furnishing the Chickasaws with weapons."

"Are any other tribes dissatisfied?"

"The Natchez."

Rouen's frown strengthened. "I don't like this, either."

"The Chickasaw raiding party took no slaves." Running Wolf signaled to his warriors to leave. "Be careful, my friend. If I find out any more information about the Englishman or the weapons, I will send a messenger."

Nodding, Rouen watched the Choctaws leave in silence.

"Running Wolf confirmed what we suspected." Claude's voice cut into the quiet.

A nerve in Rouen's jaw twitched as his narrow

gaze bored hard into the space where the Indian chief had stood only moments before.

"Suspected?" Danielle asked, her head spinning. She didn't understand any of this—the raids, the different Indian tribes, the hatred, the intrigue.

Rouen's gray eyes sharpened to steel. "We buried two children as well as a man and a woman."

For a brief moment the horror didn't register with Danielle. She instinctively tried to hold it at bay. Then all at once she was sick to her stomach, bile rising into her throat. Rushing toward the stream, she fell to her knees in the mud and threw up.

She was only half aware of Rouen kneeling behind her and placing his hands on her shoulders. She didn't care what he thought. All she could think of was what she imagined the Chickasaws had done to the children.

Tears streamed down her cheeks as she sucked in deep breaths, short sobs escaping between gulps of air. "How can people in this colony be so cruel?" She splattered cold water on her face, fighting the urge to get sick all over again.

"Claude, take Anne to the horses. We'll be along in a minute," Rouen said over his shoulder, then pulled Danielle around until she fit snugly into the shelter of his embrace. "People here are no more cruel than in France."

"But those Indians must have mutilated—" She couldn't even finish the sentence.

"No, the children weren't." His hold tightened about her. "From what you've told me about the Marquis, is he much different? He might wear different clothes and be considered civilized by most, but he has destroyed many people's lives. War brings out the savagery in people on both sides."

"But we aren't at war."

"There is a battle for the New World. One day France and England will war over this land."

"England is welcome to it."

Rouen frowned. "This colony is France's future. There is so much potential here." Cupping her face between his hands, he forced her to look up into his eyes. "There are kind people here and cruel ones. The New World is strange to you, but give it a chance. There's great beauty here that you'll never see in France."

"We'll go back to France within the year, *non?*" Panic laced her question. She couldn't bear to stay in the Louisiana Colony any longer than necessary. Her tears dampened his hands.

Sadness invaded him as he traced the wet tracks down her cheeks with a hand that trembled. "We will—as I promised." He felt as he spoke those words that he was sentencing himself to a life in a dungeon.

She tried to brush the tears away, but couldn't stop the emotional release. Rouen enveloped her in his strong arms and let her cry against his chest. She couldn't remember a time when she had been able to cry and ease the emotional strain she had felt trapped in for the past ten years. Her release melted through the ice around her emotions to the pain beneath. But even as her tears soaked his soft doeskin jacket, part of her was appalled she had given in to this weakness.

Slowly the shocked part of her grew until her tears dried. She regained the controlled calmness she had cultivated over the years to help her survive emotionally at Chateau Duchamp. Pulling away, she wiped at her tears, her shoulders thrown back, her chin at a proud angle.

"I'm fine now. We can leave." There was no emotion in her voice as she started to rise.

Rouen stopped her with a hand clasped about her waist. "Danielle, are you—"

"I can do nothing about this, nothing. We must get Anne safely back to the fort." To her own ears, she sounded cold and distant. Inside, the pit of her stomach still burned. In order to survive, though, she must shut down her emotions.

"Why are you afraid to let anyone know your feelings?"

She jerked her hand away and stood, savoring the sense of towering over him. "I am not afraid."

"You're lying, Danielle." Rouen rose and moved closer. "If not to me, to yourself. It is human to admit you need someone."

"I need no one. I rely only on myself."

"So you would have traveled to your uncle's by yourself?"

"If I'd had to, *oui.*"

"Ma petite, you are either naive or foolish."

She drew herself up straight. "I am not your little one. I may wed you, but no man will own me."

A smile slid across his lips, but left his eyes frosty. "Yes, you shall marry me. As my wife, I will expect a certain comportment. You understand, do you not, Danielle?"

"You enjoy intimidating people, *non?* Perhaps I should not be surprised now that I know your background."

"Our backgrounds are similar."

"Hardly. I was a prisoner at Chateau Duchamp."

"My point exactly. In different ways we were forced to do what we didn't want, and now we shall change that." Rouen took another step toward her. "When we marry, we can remain barely civil strangers or we can become friends."

Friends? She and Rouen? Danielle rebelled at the idea. It would give him too much power over her. She had given him more than enough by agreeing to wed him. "You do not care to be friends. Don't play me for the fool."

"You are *en garde,*" he said in a surprisingly gentle voice, void of any mockery. He drew her toward him, tilting her face up toward his. "Would it not make things easier if we liked each other?"

"For you or me?" she murmured breathlessly.

"Both of us. Do you want to live in a hostile home, like Chateau Duchamp?"

She arched a brow. "If I thought you were like the Marquis, I would rather die than marry you."

His smile was warm and melting. "A compliment, Danielle? *Merci.*"

His delicious smile eased the tension in her shoulders and neck. "I will tell you a secret, me. It was no compliment. Even that—how do you say—alligator who slithers on his belly is better than the Marquis."

Rouen threw back his head and laughed, his merriment wonderful after all that had happened to them. Danielle laughed along until tears cascaded down her cheeks. They fell together, laughing until their sides started to ache and their energy was spent.

Placing one arm about her shoulders, Rouen began walking toward the horses. "Come, we have a wedding to attend."

EIGHT

Gray mist blanketed the landscape, fingering its way between the pines and live oaks to obscure Danielle's view of Rouen's land. Pulling the folds of her cloak about her, she scanned the fog-shrouded terrain but saw only shadows. The day befitted her mood, she thought, remembering her apprehension about accompanying him to his plantation for the wedding later that day.

What do I really know of Rouen Beauvoir? she asked herself for the hundredth time in the past two days. Only what he had told her. What if he wasn't the son of a nobleman and she had to live in the New World the rest of her life? What if he were like the Marquis, polite on the surface when he wanted something but truly evil inside? What if Rouen, like Pierre, abandoned her?

The cart hit a rut in the narrow trail, jolting Danielle forward. Rouen's hand shot out to steady her and place her securely back beside him on the seat. His touch seared through the wool of her cloak, leaving the brand of his fingers on her arm. In a few hours she would be his. In the eyes of the world she would become his property, marked by her master as some slaves were. Her stomach muscles coiled tighter.

"We're almost there. I'm sorry you can't see more. The fog will burn off before the guests arrive." Rouen slanted her a warm glance, a smile deep in his eyes.

His look was meant to reassure her, but it didn't. With each mile the cart took her away from the fort and what civilization there was in this New World; her apprehension grew until her nerves were brittle, ready to shatter like glass.

"Marte has been baking and cooking these last few days." Rouen continued speaking as though it didn't matter that Danielle said nothing. "She says it's about time I settled down. She wants to see children running about the house."

The image of what it took to get children made Danielle blush. She refused to think about what would happen that evening.

"If I know Marte, she will have started making baby clothes."

"You haven't told her you're returning to France?" Danielle asked, her distrust apparent in her tone of voice.

"No, but don't worry. We'll return—as I promised. I do not go back on my word. One day you'll comprehend that." His voice and expression hardened, and he directed his full attention to the trail in front of the cart. Silence reigned between them again.

She would trust no man completely, Danielle vowed. She, too, looked straight ahead, her features set in determination. Rouen would soon discover that he would never own her in the true sense of the word.

Slowly the fog lifted until Danielle could see the cleared fields of Rouen's plantation. In the distance, the river fed into the bay. Rouen had once commented that his concession was quite a large one. They had passed no other houses on their trip from the fort. She felt very isolated in this alien world and at the mercy of its strangeness.

When they rounded a bend in the trail, she caught her first glimpse of her new home through the huge yellow pines and live oaks surrounding it. She was surprised by its size compared to other houses she had seen in the colony. With its thick walls of oyster shells, mud and moss, his home was one story with a veranda wrapping around it and a separate building for the kitchen, as well as a stable and smaller cabins in the distance, most likely for the plantation workers. As they drew closer, she noticed glass in a few of the smaller windows—a definite luxury, she had discovered, in the New World.

Rouen pulled the cart up in front of the house. "Claude and I built most of this. Through the years I've added to it—the windowpanes and the building out back for the kitchen." He jumped down and held out his arms for her. "Come, let me show you your new home before you dress for the wedding."

As he stared up at her, his hands closed about her waist, his fingers warm, possessive. That feeling of being the only two people in the world inundated Danielle again. When he swung her down, she grasped his arms, intending to step away as soon as she was on the ground. She released her grip, but he captured her hands and brought each one to his mouth, kissing the pulse in her wrists. It accelerated wildly beneath his lips. She drowned in sensations—

his mouth against her skin, the scent of pine and leather, his bent head, the deep, prolonged breath that warned of her effect on him. She could even imagine the taste of him on her lips.

"Rouen? Please," she murmured before she was totally lost to her reeling senses.

He backed away, visibly shaken as well. "Yes, the tour."

Danielle couldn't resist smiling at Rouen's eager pride as he began the tour of his home. Inside she was pleased to note the floors were covered with smooth boards and a few rugs. The parlor was a comfortable room with several pieces of furniture that had come from France. Each of the six rooms—a parlor, a dining room, an office, and three bedchambers—had a hearth and touches of France in them, like a beautifully ornamented chest. For a few minutes she felt connected to her homeland.

Rouen saved his bedchamber until last. Swinging open the door, he let Danielle enter first. The large canopy bed with ornate posts drew her immediate attention, and she didn't see anything else in the room. Its heavy blue velvet curtains were drawn back, as though inviting her to test the softness of the mattress.

"This is the only piece of furniture I had shipped over from Chateau Beauvoir."

"So you cannot completely forget France." Her voice was sharper than she intended, covering the nervousness thoughts of the bed conjured in her mind. Her gaze flitted from the chest that held his clothes to the simple hearth chairs that must have been made in the colony to the table that held a pitcher and washbasin of creamware.

He slammed the door closed and swung her around to look at him. "I think of France—often, in fact. It's my homeland, but this land is a part of France, too. Exciting things are happening here. It's our country's chance to expand, to become a power in the world. I see great possibilities for France through this colony if she'll take them."

"As do other countries. That is the reason for the Indian raids we saw, *non?* For my uncle's death?"

"Yes," Rouen answered sadly. "It won't be easy. I must make our government aware of the potential of this land. France must commit to the colony or lose it."

"And the Indians who lived here before we came? They will allow us to take their land without a fight? The raids, the horrible murders! Were they only because the English champion the Chickasaws?"

"As you champion the Indian cause?"

Danielle threw up her arms in agitation. "What am I doing? Why am I here?" She started for the door. "This whole affair is wrong. I do not wish to marry you. I do not wish to marry anyone!"

Rouen cut off her escape by leaning back against the door, his arms crossed over his chest. "You dare not back out now, Danielle. We have made a pact. Our guests arrive in an hour. Have you forgotten about Anne? About the Marquis?" A smug expression descended over his features.

She hated him in that moment. He knew she had no real choice. When they had returned to the fort, she had studied the prospective men and realized Rouen offered her the best chance to return to France and obtain her revenge. But the worst thing was he knew it, too.

"You're blackmailing me!"

His smile broadened. "No, just holding you to your word, my reluctant bride."

She laced her hands tightly together in front of her. She couldn't help the nervous patter of her heart. The other promise she had made to him concerning her wifely duties would start tonight. Looking into his eyes, she knew he thought of those duties, too.

He pushed away from the door and strode purposefully toward her. Wide eyed, she stepped back until she hit the front of the chair. He stopped inches from her, thrusting his face closer. She fell back onto the hard seat.

"You have forgotten our conversation a few days ago? Shall I refresh your memory as to the bargain you agreed to, *ma petite?*" Leaning over her, he placed a hand on each arm of the chair, trapping her there.

"You needn't remind me. Me, I have an excellent memory," she whispered. His masculine scent engulfed her until she could hardly breathe.

One thick brow rose tauntingly. "Are you sure? Perhaps you wish a taste of what is expected later."

With her body plastered against the back of the chair, she shook her head. "I prefer to wait."

A knock sounded at the bedchamber door. Danielle drew in a decent breath as Rouen straightened and bid the person enter. A robust woman came into the room, a dimpled smile of greeting on her face, a large apron covering her woolen dress.

" 'Tis time you left, Monsieur Beauvoir. Governor Bienville has arrived. *Mademoiselle* must dress. Run along." The woman waved her hands, shooing Rouen out of the bedchamber.

"Perhaps I can take lessons," Danielle said as the woman shut the door after his departure.

The woman's laugh was deep, shaking her whole body. "He's easy enough to manage when he wants to be managed."

"I find him stubborn and infuriating."

Another laugh escaped the woman. "That he is. Used to getting his own way."

"Ninety-nine percent of the time," Danielle muttered, rising from the chair. "As you no doubt know, I'm Danielle de Bussy."

"And I'm Marte Fayard. We have little time before the wedding. Monsieur Beauvoir knew you had few clothes, being one of the *casquettes,* so he asked me to make you a wedding dress." The housekeeper walked to Rouen's chest and withdrew a fine silk brocade gown of pale green, simply sewn with a squared neckline. Delicate lace trimmed sleeves that were tight to the elbow.

Danielle fingered the gown, a lump in her throat. "This is beautiful. I expected to wear this." She waved her hand down the length of her second dress of yellow wool, plainly cut with no lace or ornamentation. "What a wonderful surprise. Thank you, Marte."

The housekeeper beamed. "I would take the credit, yes, but it was Monsieur Beauvoir's idea and his material."

Ignoring the mention of Rouen, which lit a warmth deep inside her, Danielle held up the gown. "Will you help me?"

With Marte's assistance, Danielle quickly changed

into the silk brocade gown, pleased that at least for the day she wouldn't have to wear the wool dress, one of two that she owned. She thought for a moment about all the gowns she had at Chateau Duchamp. How much her life had changed in the past few months because of the Marquis. Resolved not to let the man ruin her wedding day, she pushed thoughts of France from her mind.

Holding out the skirt of the gown, Danielle whirled about the room in delight. "How in the world did you guess my exact measurements? This fits perfectly."

"Monsieur Beauvoir told me."

Danielle stopped. "He did! But—" Her voice trailed off into silence. She remembered the times he had held her intimately, and a blush tinted her cheeks.

"Perhaps you should hold thoughts of him in your mind, *mademoiselle.* It gives you a healthy glow."

Danielle was stunned at the woman's bluntness. A servant at Chateau Duchamp never would have said that to her. But she wasn't in France anymore. The sooner she realized that, the better off she would be. She needed an ally in this household.

"Sit down and I'll fix your hair." Marte indicated a chair for Danielle.

As the housekeeper piled her hair on her head, Danielle asked, "Has Anne arrived yet with Gaby?"

"I'll find out. If so, I'll send them in to you."

Danielle smiled her thanks. When Marte left, Danielle finally inspected the bedchamber she would share with Rouen. The room wasn't elaborately decorated, like Chateau Duchamp, but it was clean and fresh looking. The hearth and its fire were the main source of warmth and light. She liked its simplicity and coziness, the mixture of France and the colony, which was reflected throughout the house. That feeling surprised her. She wanted nothing to do with the New World.

"Dani! Dani!" Anne bounded into the room, throwing herself into Danielle's lap.

She hugged the small child, kissing the top of her dark hair. After Anne had recovered from the shock of the raid, she clung to Danielle, as if she sensed Danielle was to be her new mother. She still awakened every night from nightmares, and only Danielle could erase the terror.

"Did you enjoy the ride out on the horse?" Danielle asked Anne.

"Yes. I rode with Claude. He let me hold the reins."

"Would you like to learn to ride a horse?"

"Yes, Dani." Anne climbed down and began to explore the bedchamber.

Danielle looked up at Gaby, not prepared for the murderous expression on her friend's face. "What's wrong?"

"That man!"

"Who?"

"Monsieur Renoir, that's who!"

Danielle suppressed the urge to smile. "What did he do?"

"He told me to shut up! I've never—" She pinched her mouth together, too incensed to think straight. "All I did was ask a few questions about the plantation, the fort, his trip. No wonder he likes to travel in the wilderness. He's the most hostile man I've ever seen."

Anne stopped playing on the big bed and giggled. "He answered me."

Gaby's face flamed. *"Oui!* The same questions I asked! Danielle, I cannot understand how you could be with him for so long. He has the manners of a wild boar!"

"Did anything happen at the start?"

"Nothing. I was surprised that he escorted us. I thought we would come with Governor Bienville and Sister Gertrude."

"Did you tell him you were surprised?"

"But *oui."*

Danielle smiled to herself. Gaby spoke her mind. No doubt Claude took her comment to mean Gaby didn't want him to escort her because of his looks. Claude was sensitive about them, especially where women were concerned.

Danielle started to explain this to Gaby when someone knocked on the door. "Yes?"

Governor Bienville entered the room. "Everyone has arrived. Are you ready for me to escort you?"

Nervously, Danielle smoothed a hand over her brocade stomacher. Ready? Never, but she couldn't think of a good reason to postpone the wedding any longer. She was marrying Rouen for her future, for Anne. He was her way home to France. "Yes," she finally answered the governor. Gaby took Anne's hand and led her first from the chamber.

Governor Bienville held out his arm for Danielle. "I believe you two are the luckiest people in the colony today."

As she walked into the parlor, she didn't feel lucky. She felt like a prisoner walking to her death. For years she had done what the Marquis had dictated.

Now it seemed she was trading one jailer for another—granted one of her own choosing, but a jailer nonetheless.

Rouen stood at the opposite end of the room next to the traveling priest. In that moment, she believed him to be a nobleman who had frequented the court at Versailles. He wore an embroidered brocade coat with a blue satin waistcoat, a lace cravat tucked into its neck. His cream-colored stockings were worn over fitted breeches and tied with garters.

Danielle was only half aware of the other people crowded into the parlor as she walked toward Rouen. Her gaze fixed upon the man she was about to marry. He was a man of contradictions, appearing as comfortable in his elaborate dress as in doeskin jacket and pants. He could walk in two worlds and fit in each as though he belonged.

Taking her arm, Rouen drew her next to him and the priest began the wedding ceremony. Danielle dutifully answered the questions and repeated the words without mistakes, but she felt as though she performed the whole rite in a trance.

She didn't realize the ceremony was over until Rouen slipped his arms about her, pressed her against him, and kissed her, a long, deep mating of their lips that left Danielle shaken to her very core. When he released her and turned to accept the congratulations of everyone, her face was scarlet. She felt embarrassed, angry, and possessed, but couldn't hold onto a single emotion for very long.

She was pulled away from Rouen by an eager Gaby, who talked incessantly. The governor separated Rouen from the other well-wishers for a few private words.

Governor Bienville handed Rouen a glass of Madeira and raised his own in a toast. "I hope you don't live to regret your decision, *mon ami.* I hear the flower has thorns."

Rouen chuckled. "I have a high threshold for pain."

Jean-Baptiste leaned closer to whisper, "The piece of baggage you wanted transported to the river has been safely delivered."

"Monsieur Beauvoir—" Armand David approached the pair.

"Rouen, please."

"Rouen, I'm impressed with your home and plantation. You have done much in the few years you've been here."

"I hear you own a piece of property along the Mississippi near Fort Rosalie."

"Yes, I believe in the future the river will be the key to this part of the country."

"That's why I'm building Nouvelle Orleans," Governor Bienville said with his usual enthusiasm when the topic was his city on the river. "It's in the heart of the delta. Think of the possibilities when more settlers come and this land of ours expands."

"The soil is rich along the river," David said.

Rouen searched the crowd for his wife. He still had a hard time believing they were married and tonight he would satisfy his intense hunger for her. Then his life could return to normal, where his every waking thought didn't come back to Danielle.

He found her across the room next to Gaby. She looked up and their gazes became bound, just as he and Danielle were bound now in the eyes of the church, in the eyes of the law. He hardened with desire.

Danielle couldn't look away from her husband. *I'm married.* She had gone through with it. His gray gaze drilled into her, imparting a silent message of desire. She couldn't dispel the lingering stamp of ownership the man seemed to cast over her. He could do anything to her and no one would care—like her mother with the Marquis.

"Danielle, are you listening?" Gaby followed the direction of her friend's stare. "Ah, I see. Already wondering about tonight, yes?"

Danielle's attention veered sharply back to Gaby's face. "No!"

"You needn't be nervous. Personally, I wish it had been me standing before the priest with Monsieur David. Isn't he a handsome devil? It's rumored he will marry before he leaves for his plantation. He has a big house near the river. I hear it is furnished with items from France. I've been flirting with him. He would be perfect for me, *oui?*"

Danielle felt breathless by the time Gaby finished chattering about Monsieur David. But Danielle was glad her friend was with her. It took her mind off of Rouen and what he expected of her later. "I've met Monsieur David only once, Gaby. It isn't important what I think, but what you think."

"I am falling in love," Gaby declared, "and it's so much easier to fall in love with a rich man who is handsome, too." She put her hand over her breast. "My heart flutters every time I'm near him."

"That's not love," Danielle denied firmly, conscious of her own reaction when Rouen was near her.

"Desire, then. Passion."

Danielle wanted to deny that, too. She didn't desire Rouen. If she felt anything, it was indifference. *Liar.* "I know so little about Rouen. What have I gotten myself into?" She drained her wine.

"The joy in marriage is discovering each other, *oui?* You have known him less than two weeks."

"Ah, but I've bound myself to him for a lifetime. How could I have done that?"

Gaby placed her wine goblet in Danielle's hand. "You need a little more courage, Danielle. Drink this."

Danielle downed the nerve-dulling contents. When Marte passed her a few minutes later, Danielle asked her to refill the goblet. She swallowed the amber liquid quickly.

The day progressed in a blur as she listened to Rouen's neighbors and friends offer her advice and congratulations. Everyone enjoyed the rich food Marte had prepared. From the game birds to the venison to the brandied peaches and apples, Danielle hadn't seen so much to eat since she was at Chateau Duchamp.

Throughout the rest of the afternoon and early evening, she stayed on the opposite side of the room from Rouen. Occasionally she discovered him staring at her. Once he silently toasted her, then drank, measuring her over the rim of his glass. His scrutiny tethered them across the room.

She had the strange sensation he was allowing her to escape him for the time being. She felt like a mouse she had once seen caught by the cat who lived in the stables at Chateau Duchamp. The cat had toyed with the mouse, letting it think it had escaped before pouncing on it one final time and killing it. Danielle quaked at the thought.

She was exhausted both physically and mentally by the time their last guest left the house. Rouen closed the front door and turned toward her. A blaze flared in his dark gray eyes, igniting something primitive inside of her.

The air crackled with their intense emotions as Rouen moved toward her. The probing depths of his eyes mesmerized her.

"I didn't get a chance to tell you earlier how beautiful you look."

His words sped like hot buttered rum through her veins. Blood pounded in her ears as he approached her, his deliberate steps causing the tension within her to build. She had never encountered such intensity.

With only a few inches separating them, he touched her mouth, his work-toughened fingers grazing her lips. "I wanted to send the guests home hours ago." His thumb caressed her mouth; his possessive gaze lingered over her features.

Danielle's nerve endings screamed in protest. She remembered her mother crying; she remembered Bridget's stories about the act; she remembered the Marquis. Danielle froze.

"Please," she whispered hoarsely. "Don't touch me."

Rouen's eyes were like quicksilver. Irritation carved slashing lines beside his mouth. "Do you not remember our bargain?"

She nodded. *How could I have forgotten? That is all I've thought about all day.* "I don't know you."

"We will change that tonight, *ma petite.*"

He reached for her, but she pulled back. "You are still a stranger to me."

"Danielle, we must start somewhere."

"But not with . . . that."

"Damnation, woman!" With one quick movement, he anchored her to him, crushing his mouth into her soft lips.

She remained stiff in his embrace, resisting the tingling that stirred her. She must not give in to his male appeal. She must retain control.

In disgust, Rouen pushed her away from him, his thunderous expression contemptuously raking her. "I won't take a cold fish to bed, *madame.*" He stormed out of the house, slamming the door behind him.

Danielle stood trembling in the entrance hall, her arms crisscrossed over her chest. She had delayed the inevitable, but she didn't feel triumphant. She felt as though she had lost something precious and had no idea how to get it back.

NINE

Rouen stared down at his sleeping wife in the bed they should have shared the night before. Frustrated, he combed his fingers through his hair over and over, unsure what to do. He wanted her so much he hurt. She turned over and the blanket slipped lower, revealing her nightgown-clad body from the waist up. His groin tightened and it took all his will not to touch her, not to join her and take her as his body screamed for him to do.

He pivoted away and gripped the bedpost, his jaw locked till it hurt. He welcomed the pain, for it took his mind off the ache for his wife. After riding for hours, he had come to a decision. He would court Danielle, give her time to get used to him as her husband. The vulnerability he had seen in her eyes and the fear that had touched her voice the night before made him want to protect her all the more, even from himself.

He sat in the chair before the cold hearth and removed his wedding clothes. He needed to sleep even though dawn was breaking. Naked, he strode to his bed and carefully slipped under the covers, testing his will again.

He would start his campaign to win Danielle first thing when he awakened, he promised himself.

He turned his back on her delicious body, warm and inviting, her scent teasing him as he drifted off into an exhausted sleep.

Danielle snuggled into the warmth, the coldness she had felt since Rouen had left her the night before chased away by the heat radiating from—

Her eyes flew open and she gasped when she discovered herself plastered against Rouen, a naked Rouen, her arm flung over his chest, her leg over his, her face buried against his neck, his long hair mingling with hers. His male scent rendered her weak with desire.

Maybe she could slip from his embrace without his knowing. She carefully lifted her leg from his. Raising her head, she found herself staring into Rouen's pearl-gray eyes. Her heart pounded a mad staccato against her breast. Words failed her as he trapped her with his sensuous look.

"Good morning, Danielle," he murmured, a smile gracing his mouth.

She couldn't tear her gaze away. When he smiled, his whole face lit up and his eyes gleamed with silver lights. Heat flooded her body. She dropped her glance to the cleft in his chin, hoping to clear her mind.

"Some say that is the mark of the devil." She traced the dent in his chin with her finger, desperately trying to turn all her attention to any part of his body that didn't make hers feel like liquid heat.

"There are people who might agree that is true about me."

"C'est vrai?" Her gaze returned to his, her hand slipping away from his face.

"It isn't easy carving a home out of the wilderness. But I won't hurt you, *ma petite.* I will give you the time you need to get used to having a husband." He smiled again. "Just don't make me wait too long. I'm not a patient man."

He lightly kissed her lips, then slid from the bed. Though he was naked, Danielle couldn't look away from him as he walked to the chest and selected buckskin breeches and a muslin shirt to wear. Her cheeks burned as she admired his magnificent body. Tall and muscled from hard, physical labor, he could take what he wanted from her. But he hadn't last night, though she had promised him she would be a wife in every sense.

When he turned toward her, she glanced at the hearth. She felt his regard on her and her blush deepened. What kind of man had she married? He wasn't like the Marquis or Pierre. She suspected he was like no other man.

"I'll have Marte serve us breakfast in the dining room," he said from the doorway, then left her alone to get dressed.

How could she share a bedchamber with him—a bed? She scrambled from under the blankets and hurried to put on her blue wool dress, stockings, and shoes. She would insist on separate bedchambers.

In the dining room, she paused in the doorway and watched Rouen feeding Anne, who sat on his lap. He glanced up and his look snared hers. The scene transfixed her. Anne giggled and pulled on

Rouen's hair, which he hadn't tied back yet. It hung about his shoulders like a thick black curtain.

"Here. Let me finish feeding her." Danielle moved to take Anne from Rouen.

"She's fine where she is. Sit down and eat."

"But she is my responsibility."

"No, Danielle, she is *our* responsibility. I gave my word to Running Wolf that I would protect and care for Anne, and I will."

Her husband's words touched her heart, constricting her throat with emotions she had buried slowly over the years she had lived at Chateau Duchamp. She sat next to him, her back to the fire, then lavished butter on a thick piece of bread and poured tea into her cup. Though Rouen's plate held smoked fish, preserved peaches, and cheese, she knew she couldn't eat much. Tension knotted her stomach.

Marte entered the dining room and whisked Anne from Rouen's arms. "She needs a bath."

Danielle started to rise. "Then I will—"

"I will see to Anne's bath. You sit and talk with your husband." Marte hurried out of the room.

Taking her seat again, she stared at her tea. "Is there a bedchamber I can move my things to?"

"No. You will share mine—as you will share everything that is mine."

Looking up at him, she understood the determined set to his jaw meant he would not give in on this. Thoughts of them in bed together heightened the color in her face. "Do you always sleep—" She swallowed several times.

"I sleep in my clothes only on the trail."

The amusement in his voice caused her to narrow

her gaze and frown. "Then I will start making you a nightshirt after I eat."

"Don't bother. I won't wear it." Laugh lines deepened the creases at the corners of his eyes.

"You cannot expect me to sleep with a man who is . . . naked."

"I can and I do. When we make love, Danielle, you will want it as much as I."

She could never imagine that. "I know we must from time to time in order to give you an heir."

"You have nothing to fear from me." He tilted his head to the side. "Do you know what goes on between a man and a woman?"

Her cheeks burned as if she were standing too close to the flames behind her. She resisted fanning herself and instead gripped her hands together in her lap. "Of course."

"What do you know?"

She shot to her feet, her body fiery with embarrassment, with visions of them making love on the table before her. "Excuse me."

She fled the room, escaping to the bedchamber she shared with him. She had no other place to go. She closed the door and paced, her pulse thundering against her temples, her chest rising and falling rapidly. She couldn't shake the image of them wrapped together, skin against skin, lips against lips.

The door opened and Rouen stood in the entrance, filling it with his masculine presence. The strength siphoned from Danielle's legs. She sank onto the bed, her whole body hot and trembling as though heated brandy fingered outward to every part of her. She didn't understand what was happening to her.

He closed the door and leaned back against it, crossing his arms over his chest, his gaze boring into her with an intensity that stole her breath. "What do you know, Danielle? Why are you so afraid?"

She straightened, lifting her chin, and met his intent regard with an unwavering one. "I know a woman must endure the act of—of copulating. It is my duty as a wife, one I promised you I would fulfill, and I will. I just—I need some time."

"*Mon Dieu,* woman, where did you learn this?"

"Bridget told me."

"Who is Bridget?"

"My stepfather's mistress. She lives at the chateau."

"You turned to her to learn about making love?"

Danielle stiffened at the incredulous tone of his voice. "Who would you have me ask? My mother? I knew what she had to endure. Sister Mary Catherine was the only other woman I knew. Oh, and some of the maids at the chateau. The Marquis would use them when he tired of my mother or Bridget. He particularly liked to see them cry or scream. There were times late at night when I couldn't sleep because of the sounds they made."

Suddenly she no longer felt hot but cold, icy memories inundating her. She hugged her arms to her and rubbed them, trying to ward off the chill lancing into her as his possessive gaze had moments before.

Rouen moved with lightning speed across the room and pulled her to her feet. He dragged her into his embrace and wrapped his arms around her as though to draw the cold from her and into him. "You know very little, *ma petite.* When we make love, you will enjoy it as much as I. There will be nothing for you to endure."

She wanted to believe him—almost did—but she could still remember her mother's sobs after the Marquis had left. "I have seen the Marquis take my mother." She shuddered with the memory.

"I am nothing like the Marquis. Don't ever mistake me for him."

She looked up into his face. "I could not have wed you had I thought that."

"Your body will welcome mine. Before we are through, you will plead for me to take you. I will have it no other way."

She kept her doubts to herself; she could never imagine pleading for that.

His thumb brushed across her lips. "You don't believe me. I realize nothing I say will change your mind."

Before she could respond, Rouen slanted his mouth over hers, his tongue pushing inside to savor her. For a few seconds, her mind went blank, then sensations flooded it—the feel of him against the length of her, hard against soft; the smell of him surrounding her. He tasted sweet; his whiskers felt rough. The world spun as he scooped her up into his arms, never breaking his kiss, and placed her gently on the bed. He rested beside her, framing her face within his large hands.

The glitter of desire in his eyes robbed her of rational thought. She parted her lips and ran her tongue over his lingering taste. He sucked in a sharp breath and brought his mouth down on hers again, driving her into the moss-stuffed mattress.

"*Ma petite,* you will not regret this."

She felt light-headed, everything swirling like a whirlpool, drawing her down and down into sensations that left her weak and wanting so much more.

When his hand covered her breast, she arched up into the touch, pinpricks of pleasure spreading from her center outward to every inch of her body. She wanted to feel, to experience something beyond her ken.

The sound of her gown ripping sobered her. She had heard that sound often when the Marquis used one of the maids for his pleasure. Soon cries and screams would follow. She stiffened in Rouen's embrace.

He drew back, a frown creasing his brow, a question in his eyes.

"You promised to give me time."

For a long moment he held himself over her while a battle raged inside him. She saw the emotions come and go in his expression and held her breath, expecting him to continue tearing the clothes from her body. Then suddenly he retreated, barricading his emotions.

Rouen sat up and pulled the pieces of Danielle's bodice together to cover her breasts. "I only meant to show you some of what can transpire between a man and a woman. I went too far." He stared at the bedchamber door. "I will not lie to you, Danielle. I want you. I promised you I would wait until you're ready, but my will is only so strong."

She should be alarmed at his warning, but she couldn't forget what she had experienced for a short time in his arms. Maybe she had been wrong about making love. She no longer knew what to believe.

"You're right. It would be better if I sleep in another bedchamber." Rouen rose and gathered some of his things. "I'll have Marte get the rest later."

As he headed for the door, Danielle said, "Please don't leave. This is your bedchamber." The sensations still lingered, and she wanted to explore them further. She had to stop running from what she must do as his wife. She had faced many things over the past few months; she could face this, too.

"If I stay, I can't guarantee we won't repeat this."

"I know." She sat up, holding the edges of her gown together. He had stopped when she had asked him to, as the Marquis would not. Rouen had to be different.

He stared at her for a long moment, then walked to his chest and replaced his clothing. Rouen moved without a wasted motion. The heat pooled again in the pit of her stomach.

When he turned toward her, he frowned. "I'm sorry about the gown. I know how hard it is to get material here in the colony. Another ship from France should arrive soon with supplies on it. Perhaps you can get some material to make a dress to replace this one."

"I shall mend this one."

"You need more clothes than you have. My wife will not wear rags."

Danielle laughed. "After weeks at sea and a trip through the wilderness, I think you have accurately described this gown."

"Do you have something you can wear to ride in?"

"I have the yellow wool."

"Good. I want to show you Riverview Plantation. Be ready to leave in thirty minutes."

From the proud tone in his voice, she knew it

would be hard for Rouen to leave what he had built to return to France. For herself, she could leave right now and never think once about the colony. "What about Anne?"

"Marte has insisted she will take care of her. She feels we need some privacy."

"Rouen, Anne needs me. I must spend some time with her, or she will think I have deserted her, too."

At the door, he glanced back at her. "We will be gone no more than two hours. Then you can spend the rest of the day with Anne. I have business at the fort later today."

When Rouen left, Danielle remained seated on the bed for a few minutes, her thoughts troubled and confused. So many things were new to her, things that challenged what she had believed for so long. She didn't know what to think or feel anymore.

Rouen urged his stallion forward and Danielle followed him. Splashes of green added a vivid dash of color to the bleak winter, and she craned her neck to look at the towering pine trees that lined the trail.

Rouen pointed to a clear patch of land. "Next spring that will be planted with indigo." He waved his arm toward another barren field. "Rice will be there in a few months." As they neared the river, he indicated lowlands that would be used to plant maize. "I don't believe in having only one crop. Too many things can go wrong."

Danielle heard water lapping against the shore. Halting her mare beside Rouen's stallion, she looked across the stretch of fields to a line of trees and the glint of water.

"My plantation is on the river that feeds into the bay."

She lifted her face to the sun's rays and relished their warmth. A light breeze blew off the water, and she breathed deeply of the salt-saturated air. "This is beautiful. So primitive. You have so much land still left untouched."

"A man can feel free working his land here in the colony."

"Isn't that why you have slaves?"

"My workers earn wages." His gaze captured hers. "I have worked alongside them to build the house, to sow the fields." The laugh lines at the corners of his eyes deepened as he grinned. "I didn't mean to preach to you. Some men in the colony don't believe I'm doing things the right way."

"You don't care about what others think?"

"I care about what some think—the ones who deserve my respect and friendship."

"Like Governor Bienville?"

"He's one of them. He has visions for this colony that I agree with."

"Visions?"

"Like the city he is building on the Mississippi River. He thinks it will be an important port one day." Rouen scanned the terrain around him. "I know this place doesn't have what most people call civilization, but it's limited only by our imagination."

"You should have been an explorer." Her stomach rumbled and she realized she hadn't eaten much earlier. Now she was hungry.

"Marte packed us some food. I know a clearing not far from here."

Danielle kicked her horse into action and galloped behind Rouen through a clump of trees until they reached the clearing. A stream flowed through a glade filled with live oaks dripping Spanish moss, tall pines that towered above the landscape, and a tree she didn't know. She could almost believe winter had passed. All the trees were leafed out and there was green everywhere.

"I've never seen that tree before. What is it?" She pointed to the broad, thick leaves of one tree.

"A magnolia. They have fragrant white blossoms in the warm months. There is no better place in the spring."

"I can almost believe its springtime now."

He dismounted his stallion and came over to her. With his hands on her waist he helped her down, but he didn't release his hold. She looked up into his face and became lost in the intensity in his eyes.

"I'm going to kiss you, *ma petite.*"

The husky timbre to his voice made her quiver. He gently nipped at her lower lip. The teasing produced a tightening in her stomach, and she waited in anticipation for what she now knew would follow. When he finally took her mouth in a deep kiss, she clutched at his shoulders to steady herself. He pulled her against him, his arms enveloping her, his strength surrounding her and holding her upright.

When he ended the kiss, he rested his forehead against hers. "It is so damned hard to keep my hands off you."

His words thrilled her. She shouldn't be pleased—in fact, she should be worried he wouldn't keep his promise—but she wasn't. Part of her wanted him to take her right here in the glade. Shocked at her train of thought, she backed away from him and pretended to busy herself with an inspection of the clearing.

Rouen spread the blanket on the ground and set out the wine and food. Lounging back as though he had not a care in the world, he cut chunks of cheese and tore off pieces of bread. He made Danielle's heart flutter, her pulse gallop.

Rouen indicated she join him on the blanket and handed her a goblet of malmsey. She immediately drank half the contents. He looked at the glass, then at her, his gaze heavy lidded as it slowly traveled down her body. She wanted to melt from the luscious feelings swirling inside her. He had a way of making a woman feel as if she were the only one in the world.

"Tell me about Chateau Beauvoir, your family."

"As you know, my older brother died recently. I have no other siblings. My mother died when I was fourteen. My father never remarried."

"And he wants you to return home and marry?"

"Yes, to a wife he has already picked out." Rouen drank some of his wine, watching her over the rim of his glass.

"What do you think he will do when he finds out about me?"

"He will not be happy. He thinks his duty is to pick my wives for me. I think differently. Besides, *we* are married."

"But he could be difficult?" She thought about the Marquis and didn't want to have to deal with a man like him, even if it was her father-in-law, not her husband.

"You needn't worry. He will rant and rave for a

few days, then accept you because he has no other choice. My father is practical, if nothing else."

"When are you going to tell him?"

"The day I arrive with you at Chateau Beauvoir."

"Is it possible he will find out sooner?"

"Possibly." Rouen downed the rest of his drink and took a bite of some cheese and bread. "Tell me about your stepfather."

"There isn't much more to say. The Marquis is evil. My mother didn't discover that until it was too late. After my father died, she wed the first man who asked her. She was afraid to be alone."

"Your stepfather does not know you are in the colony?"

"No. I would not be here if he did. No one crosses him and lives to tell about it."

A nerve in Rouen's jaw twitched as he stared at her. He gripped the knife he was using to cut the cheese. "Then he has met his match. No one will harm my family."

For the first time since her father's death, Danielle felt safe and protected. Tears clogged her throat, and she had to fight to keep them at bay. She had wanted Pierre to say those words, but he had left her to the mercy of the Marquis, forcing her to flee for her life. She understood why—and yet she didn't. Part of her had wanted him to stand up to the Marquis no matter what.

Rouen reached across the space separating them and smoothed the creases from her brow. "You are safe, Danielle. I promise. Don't worry about the Marquis. He will rue the day he tried to rape you."

She needed to be invincible, but when he spoke like that, he appealed to her soft side. Again she swallowed hard several times and looked away to disguise her tears. For ten years she had lived with very little hope. Suddenly she felt faith in the human race, all because of Rouen Beauvoir.

Danielle opened the front door and stared into the darkness beyond the house, wondering where Rouen was. He had gone to the fort earlier and should have been back. She remembered the Indian raids, remembered the man called Delon dying at her feet. Her fear escalated. What if something happened to Rouen? What if he were lying on the trail hurt—or worse, dead? Her fear spiked, making her mouth go dry and her palms sweat.

Again she searched the night, but saw no sign of Rouen. When had she come to depend on him so much? The question took her by surprise. She would not permit him that much control over her. The Marquis had ruled every aspect of her mother's life—every aspect of *her* life. That would never happen to her again.

A cry pierced the air, sending shivers through her. Danielle whirled about and snatched up the candle she had placed on a nearby table. Another cry made her run as though the hounds of hell nipped at her heels.

She thrust open the door into Anne's room, the candlelight flickering into the darkness. Its rays threw eerie shadows across the walls.

"Maman! Papa!"

The words twisted her insides. She, more than anyone, understood Anne's nightmare. Danielle rushed to the bed and scooped the child into her arms, taking her to the lone wooden chair in the room.

As Danielle rocked back and forth, she whispered soothing woods to Anne as the child's tears soaked her nightgown.

Danielle began a lullaby that her mother used to sing to her when her father was alive and they had been a happy family. She wished she could absorb the child's pain, but knew she couldn't. Slowly the cries subsided and Anne relaxed.

As she held her cousin, Danielle vowed Anne would have a good life, would have the advantages of a child born in France—things she would have had if Robert hadn't been forced from his homeland by the Marquis. Danielle never wanted Anne to witness violence again. Somehow Danielle must convince Rouen to leave the colony as soon as possible.

For a few more minutes, she held Anne in her arms and she tried to come up with an argument that would persuade Rouen to alter his plans. Scene after scene played across Danielle's mind as she, too, relived the horror of the raids. Tension twisted its way through her body like a vine in the swamp, and she knew she had to lay Anne down before the child sensed her anxiety.

Rising, she moved toward the bed and halted halfway across the room. Rouen stood framed in the doorway, looking capable of protecting her from anyone who wanted to do her harm. Her heart sped. She could take only shallow breaths as she placed Anne in her bed and quietly walked toward her husband of a day.

He remained in the doorway, blocking her way. "Another nightmare?"

She nodded, her throat tight from emotions she

had fought to keep hidden. The horrors were always there.

He took the candle from her and led her toward their bedchamber. She followed as though in a trance, the images of the Indians torturing the settler tormenting her.

When Rouen closed the door on the outside world, Danielle tried to erase the picture from her mind. She couldn't. She had run from thinking about it. She could run no more. The trembling started in her hands and quickly spread. Standing in front of the warm fire, she clasped her arms to her, but nothing stopped her body from quaking.

Rouen came up behind her, his arms encircling her and pulling her back against him. "You and Anne are safe now."

His whispered reassurance warmed her, yet she trembled as though cold had embedded itself deep inside her. "I can't stop thinking about my uncle and that settler. I don't know if I ever will forget those screams."

"I won't." His hold tightened about her.

She felt his strength and drew from it, part of her realizing that she needed to, part of her wishing she didn't. "Please, let's leave now."

He stiffened.

"I know you want to stay another year, but what if those Indians raid this place?"

"You are safe."

She turned within his embrace and looked up into his face. "Why do you stay and put yourself in danger? You have so much in France."

He released her and stepped back. "You think if we return to France nothing bad will happen to us?"

"Yes."

The line of his jaw strengthened, a nerve jerking. "I won't spend the next year arguing with you over this. We made a bargain. You will abide by it."

The finality in his voice prodded her anger. Suddenly she wanted to hurt him. "What are you afraid of in France? What are you running from?"

His eyes narrowed, his hands clenched.

"Your father? The woman he wants you to marry, your brother's wife?"

"Leave Liliane out of this."

"You were in love with her, weren't you?" She tried to keep the quiver from her voice, but it laced each word.

He unclenched his hands, spreading his fingers wide before fisting them again. "Only the truth will stand between us. Yes, I was in love with Liliane. She married my brother because he was to inherit the estate and title."

"Then why didn't you return to France and marry her?"

"My father will never rule my life again. My wife died because she was forced into a marriage she didn't want and was unsuited for."

"You still love Liliane, *non?*"

"Love complicates. I love no one."

With a great deal of effort Danielle hid her disappointment. His declaration only confirmed what she already knew. If she lost her heart to this man, she would be hurt. She must not come to depend on him for anything. Both had reasons not to love. "I must agree. People act the fool when they are in love."

"Do you not love Pierre?"

"Pierre holds a special place in my heart. We were childhood friends." She decided in that moment to dwell on the good times she and Pierre had, rather than that last evening. He'd had as little control of his life as she'd had of hers.

The room filled with tension. Danielle turned her back on her husband and stretched her cold hands toward the warm fire. The heat did nothing to chase away the chill that encased her. "I still don't understand why we can't leave this place soon. You are safe from Liliane and your father. We are married."

Silence greeted her statement.

She glanced over her shoulder and wished she hadn't. His angry features told her she had pushed him too far. She looked back at the fire.

He gripped her and whirled her about. "Yes, we are married, aren't we? Should I take what is rightly mine?"

She lifted her head, intending to tell him what she thought. His mouth came down on hers, driving her back. If he hadn't been holding her, she would have fallen. Fear gripped her, but his kiss softened into a gentle persuasion and made her tremble worse than the horrific images of the raids had.

Cupping her face, he trailed tiny nibbles to her earlobe and nipped at its shell. She felt her fears fade as the wanton woman inside pushed forward. Her arms imprisoned him as she returned his kisses. Her hands explored his muscular body.

He lifted her into his arms and headed for the bed. Depositing her upon its softness, he straightened, his gaze locking with hers. "If I made love to you now, I would face your wrath in the morning.

When you come to me, there will be no regrets." He strode toward the door. "Good night, *madame.*"

Again she was left alone to try and sleep while her body ached with a need she couldn't define. She felt rejected and wanted all at the same time. She knew enough to realize Rouen wanted her as a man wanted a woman. Then she thought of the Marquis and she was reminded of the power of sex. Remembering how the Marquis would use her mother, then reject her, Danielle understood Rouen's lust meant little. As the fire died, she hardened her heart toward her husband. She was not chattel, something to be used at her husband's whim, then discarded.

TEN

Danielle watched Anne play with her new doll, carved by Claude out of a piece of oak and clad in a dress Marte had sewn from bits of material. After an active day of trying to keep up with Anne, it was nice to sit for a few minutes and relax. Danielle sighed. "Claude and Marte spoil Anne."

"She is such a beautiful, sweet child. How can one not want to hug her and never let her go?" Gaby, too, watched Anne, who sat on the wooden floor in front of the parlor hearth.

"She has my uncle's eyes. When I look into them I remember . . . I used to sit on his lap and listen for hours to the stories he would tell me. He had a gift with words, and he loved adventure. This New World suited him."

"As it does not you?"

Danielle stared at the yellow brocade she was sewing into a gown for herself. The lines would be simple, with little decoration. She had to be practical now. Before, in France, she had never considered sewing a gown or what style it needed to be. That had always been done for her. Thankfully Marte was skilled with a needle and was helping her with this gown. "No, I was raised in a far different world."

Not even with Gaby would Danielle talk about her life in France.

"Life here is much different than at the convent. But the nuns taught me all the necessary skills—cooking, sewing, planting a kitchen garden, cleaning."

None of which Danielle was equipped to do. But she was also learning to cook from Marte and soon she would help plant a kitchen garden. These tasks, as well as keeping up with Anne, were a blessing. They occupied her mind, and at the end of the day she would fall into bed—the one she shared with her husband—exhausted.

"You may need none of them if you wed Monsieur David," she said, quickly turning her thoughts away from Rouen. "His plantation on the Mississippi is said to be large and staffed with many slaves."

Gaby's eyes twinkled. "When he describes his new house, it sounds so beautiful. He is determined to bring civilization to the New World, beginning with his home."

"Do you love him? Care for him?"

"He has so much to offer me."

"What do you know of him?"

"He's rich. He's handsome. He's always the gentleman around me. Do you know, he hasn't even kissed me yet!"

Danielle's own memories stirred. Since that night four weeks before when Rouen had placed her on the bed after thoroughly kissing her, he hadn't kissed her again and had only touched her when necessary. It made her crazy. The more she was around him, the more the knot in her stomach grew, tension spreading outward and stretching her nerves to their limit.

"And what about your marriage, Danielle? I've been here an entire day and I've seen your husband only once."

"Rouen has been busy preparing the fields for spring planting. He and Claude even sup with the workers." And her husband was avoiding her, Danielle thought, and picked up the sleeve of her gown to sew some lace on its cuff. "This last week, Rouen has come in late each night and fallen into bed exhausted. Each morning he has been gone before I wake." She had missed seeing her husband to the point that the day before last she had ridden out to the field just to get a glimpse of him. She had tried not to let him see her, but Marte said Rouen had known she was watching him.

"Perhaps that will end soon. On my walk out here, I noticed the fields were almost ready. Claude was removing some tree stumps from one of them."

A stiffness in Gaby's voice prodded Danielle to ask, "What did he have to say to you?"

Gaby looked away. "Not much. He doesn't talk much."

"What's wrong?"

"He wasn't completely clothed. I didn't know where to look! It's been unusually hot for the end of February, but he had removed his shirt!" Gaby waved her hand in front of her face as though she were hot and she needed to cool off.

"And?"

"And he was sweating. His back—it was glistening in the sun." Gaby returned her gaze to Danielle, her eyes wide as if still astonished a day later. "He has many muscles. Have you seen his arms?"

"He likes physical work. So does Rouen." When

Danielle had seen her husband in the field, he had been wearing his shirt, but the damp material clung to the muscles that rippled across his back. She could easily picture Rouen without a shirt, his back glistening in the sun, his muscles bulging. Her pulse raced with the vision imprinted on her mind, with the memories of how she had reacted to him working alongside the others, hefting the ax over and over as he chopped down a small oak tree. Danielle tried to contain her emotions, but she had to put down her needle and material because her hands were damp.

"Well, he shouldn't work unclothed. I told him it was indecent."

"You did?"

"*Oui.* And he said it was indecent for a woman to leave the fort alone. I told him it was none of his business; I chose to visit my friend for a few days."

"Is that why Claude escorted you to the house? I was surprised, because I knew he hadn't gone to the fort."

"He insisted, though I hadn't far to go. That man is—is *overbearing.* I tried to walk ahead of him, to not carry on a conversation."

"Men think they know what is best."

"*C'est vrai.* He lectured me! For a man of few words, he said much about my going out alone. He has insisted on escorting me back to the fort when I leave. Well, I will not let him know when I leave."

"He'll know."

"You would tell him?" Panic entered Gaby's voice.

"I won't have to. He'll know. He has eyes in the back of his head, that one."

"*Oui.* It is quite daunting."

"I know. Rouen may not be around the house, but he knows what is going on. He knew about Anne climbing on the stool and falling off. He knew about me chasing that mouse with the broom."

"So I must suffer Claude's escort all the way to the fort?"

" 'Twill not be so bad. Truth told, I'm glad. I don't want you walking alone from the fort, either." Danielle knew firsthand the violence that reigned. Gaby deserved a good life, a safe life. She was so kindhearted and warm. Danielle prayed the man her friend wed would treat her well. "I'm glad for your visit, but why did you leave without an escort?"

"Armand is gone for a week and Monsieur Pinart makes my skin crawl."

"Mine, too. Has he settled on a bride?"

"In time he will. He has more to offer than most, and at the fort there are too many people, too little food."

"You're welcome to stay while Armand is gone. Does Sister Gertrude know where you are?"

"I told Marie to tell her. If I had asked her leave, she would have said no."

Danielle laughed. "If you marry Monsieur David, things should be interesting for him. You have such life in you."

"Will your husband join us for dinner tonight?"

"Yes, he told Marte to expect him and Claude. She is preparing a feast."

"Claude too?"

"He often eats with us. Why?" Danielle put her gown aside and went to Anne, who had curled up on the floor with her doll pulled to her chest and was sound asleep.

"It is nothing."

"Claude would make a wonderful father." Danielle lifted Anne into her arms and came back to sit next to Gaby.

Gaby coughed, her face reddening. "Claude, a father! He must be a husband first."

"True." Adjusting Anne in her arms so the child's cheek was cradled against her breasts, Danielle lowered her head to hide her smile. When Gaby and Claude were together, sparks flew. "Anne adores him. He and Rouen fight over who will play with her in the evening. Anne has missed them this past week. At least she will be happy to see them."

"Oh, I'll be happy to see Rouen."

"But not Claude?"

"If that man says one word about—"

"About what?"

Gaby gasped and glanced toward the door. Claude stood inside the entrance, scowling. "None of your business."

Danielle looked past Claude to Rouen. Her husband's dark gray eyes seemed to penetrate her. She swallowed several times and held Anne tighter. His entrance always overwhelmed her senses. She felt more alive when he came into a room, and that reaction alarmed her. She didn't want to need anyone for anything, yet that was exactly what was happening.

"If you're talking about walking around by yourself, then it certainly is my business."

Gaby leaped to her feet. "By whose order, *monsieur?*"

Claude strode into the parlor until he was dangerously close to Gaby. "Mine."

Gaby opened her mouth, but no words came out. She snapped her mouth closed, her eyes stormy and her hands fisted. With Anne in her arms, Danielle struggled to stand so she could move between Gaby and Claude if necessary. Rouen appeared at her side and took the child from her.

"Maybe we should let them settle it on their own," he whispered to Danielle.

Gaby stepped forward until only inches separated her and Claude. "Nothing about me is your business. I will not be treated like a child."

"When you act like one, you will be treated like one." Claude's voice rose in volume.

Anne stirred in Rouen's arms, her whimper filling the tension-fraught silence. Claude glanced at them and his scowl strengthened.

"See what you made me do, woman? I almost woke up Anne because of your foolish notion you are a man," Claude whispered in a furious tone.

"A man!" Gaby's voice equaled his volume and fervor. "I have no such illusions. If you had looked at me lately, you would know that!"

Claude backed away and let his heated inspection travel down the length of her. A nerve near his scar twitched as his gaze flared. "Good. Then there will be no going back to the fort on your own." He stalked from the parlor before Gaby could reply.

"The nerve of that one," she sputtered. "I will help Marte with dinner. Maybe there is more bread to knead. I feel like pounding something."

When Gaby left the parlor, Danielle shook her head. "Tonight should be interesting."

She turned toward Rouen and her breath caught. He was rocking Anne before the hearth, smoothing her hair away from her face, whispering soothing words. A sudden yearning swelled inside of Danielle. She wanted him to touch her like that, softly, as though he cherished her above all else. She wanted him to whisper tender words to her.

"Gaby shakes Claude up. He suggested we come in early to clean up for dinner. Who might he want to impress? Not us."

"Oh, my. He likes her?" Danielle asked, determined to forget she wanted her husband. Once that happened, she wouldn't be her own person.

"Claude has shown no interest in women since I've known him. He said he's missed playing with Anne. He made a point of telling me that several times."

"I'll see to Anne while you clean up." Danielle sat in the chair Gaby had been using.

Standing, Rouen brought the child to Danielle and settled her in her arms, but he didn't move away. He looked down at Danielle, watching her as she positioned Anne to make the child more comfortable. "Anne is lucky to have you. You're very good with her."

The warmth of his words suffused her. She glanced up and was seized by his smoldering regard. Her insides constricted; her heartbeat sped up. "Thank you. She is an easy child to love. If only I could wipe away her pain."

Rouen reached out and curled a stray strand of Danielle's hair around his finger. "All parents wish that. All we can do is cherish her. She isn't waking as much with nightmares. That's a good sign."

"Because she is so active during the day. I wish I had half her energy."

Rouen released the curl but trailed his hand down her cheek, his touch infinitely soft. "Claude is almost finished making her that rocking horse. Just in time—she already wants to ride a real horse." He smiled, cupping the side of her face. "And now I must bathe so I don't offend Gaby—and Claude."

Danielle watched him walk from the room, feeling strangely bereaved that he was no longer touching her. She didn't understand these odd sensations she experienced when she was around him. She didn't want to make love to Rouen. Then why was he all she could think about?

Damn, but Danielle was all he could think about. Rouen poured the last bucket of hot water into the wooden tub and stepped in. He had found a ribbon on the floor and had grown hard, immediately picturing Danielle wearing only that ribbon in her hair, beckoning him. If he didn't make love to her soon, he would have to plan a long trip into the wilderness or he wouldn't be able to keep his promise to give her time.

Rouen lathered his body, scrubbing away the dirt and grime of the fields. He was sure after they made love he wouldn't want to rip off her clothes and take her whenever he was with her. He often worked in the fields, but lately he had stayed longer than usual until he was so tired all he could do was fall into bed at night.

This past week had been hell. The more he was with her, the more he wanted her. It was becoming painful. He had never thought a slip of a woman could test his patience as thoroughly as Danielle, but in his heart he knew she wasn't ready to give herself completely to him, and that was what he wanted most.

Sinking down into the warm water until it covered most of his body, Rouen rested his head on the lip of the tub and closed his eyes. Instantly a picture of his wife materialized in his mind. He would be crazy before this was over.

Danielle opened the door to her bedchamber, intending to get her shawl from her chest before dinner. She stopped just inside the room. Her husband was sound asleep in a tub of cold water. Her heart paused for a few seconds, then resumed its pace, its tempo quick. She turned to flee before he awoke. Her reaction to him when he was dressed was bad enough. When he wore no clothes, she just wasn't herself.

"Don't leave on my account."

His words halted her in mid-stride. She squeezed her eyes closed for a moment, then drew in a deep breath and spun toward him. "I thought you had finished with your bath."

He smiled, a slow uplifting of the corners of his mouth. "No doubt, or you wouldn't be here." He stood, water dripping from his magnificent, perfectly proportioned body. "As you see, I hadn't." He gestured toward a piece of cloth draped over the chair by the fire. "Will you hand that to me?"

Danielle stood rooted to the spot, her gaze widening. He grew harder with each moment that passed. She couldn't look away, though she needed to move to end this sweet torture.

"*Madame,* if you don't care to start what you cannot finish, I suggest you hand me something to cover myself."

She mentally shook herself and rushed forward, snatching up the cloth and thrusting it at him. She turned her full attention on the flames leaping in the hearth. They rivaled the heat in her cheeks. "I came for my shawl. I'll retrieve it and leave you to dress."

"As I said, don't leave on my account. Come, tell me about your day while I dress." Climbing from the tub, Rouen dried himself, then knotted the cloth about his waist.

Opening her chest, he removed her shawl and placed it over her shoulders. His hands lingered on her, his fingers kneading the muscles that tightened whenever he was near. "What troubles you, *ma petite?* You're as tight as an Indian's bowstring."

She shook her head, wishing she could lean back into him and let him massage her whole body, to put an end to her torment. His fingers could work magic, she thought, and relished the feel of them easing her shoulders and neck.

"How did you spend your day?"

"Gaby and I helped Marte in the kitchen baking the loaves of bread we will need this week. Of course, Anne demanded much of my time, and I'm working on a gown when I can." Everything sounded so wifely that for a moment she was stunned. When had she become a wife in every sense except one?

"Shall we have some tonight?"

His whispered question pulled her away from her musing and reminded her that she was alone with her husband and he was wearing very little. She felt hot. She no longer needed the shawl that had brought her to the bedchamber. Instead, she wanted to remove her clothing before she began to perspire.

"Danielle?"

"Oh, yes, we will have one of the loaves," she finally managed to say, her mind dwelling on the fact that Rouen was a fine male specimen. His hands still rested on her shoulders, but they had ceased any movement. She felt the length of him along her back. Sweat beaded her upper lip.

"Good. For someone who knew little about cooking before coming here, you've learned much in a short time."

His compliment made the fluttering of her heart increase. "This isn't like Chateau Duchamp. There's so much to do. Everyone must work here."

He squeezed her shoulders. "We work together."

"You make it sound like we are partners."

Turning her to face him, he lifted her chin. "We are, Danielle. That is marriage."

"Not what I know of marriage."

"The Marquis is a model for the devil." Rouen framed her face with his hands. "My father might have dictated my life, but when my mother was alive, he always consulted her about major and minor decisions."

"As you will consult me?" She heard the challenge in her voice but didn't care. She didn't believe him.

"Yes."

"But you didn't about returning to France."

"When we agreed to marry, that was part of our bargain—along with several other things."

His hot look drilled into her, vividly reminding her of one of those "other things." She wouldn't be able to stave him off much longer. Perhaps she no longer wanted to. She was tense when she was around him, as if she awaited something that never happened.

She dropped her gaze to his throat. "Should we take care of those other things?" Her voice quavered. She felt the corded tension in his hands and glanced up into his eyes. They singed her.

Slowly the tension siphoned from him, and he smiled. "No, you're not ready."

For a few seconds, she longed to scream. Frustration churned in her stomach. "It must be done. What's there to be ready for?"

His chuckle was low, a sensuous sound. "If you have to ask, then you're not ready, *ma petite.* I want no regrets when we make love."

"What if I'm never ready, as you put it? You want children, *non?*"

His hands slipped from her face and he stepped back. *"Mon Dieu!* Don't test me, Danielle. I want a marriage like my parents had, based on respect and friendship. If you do something you don't want, how will we arrive at that?"

She pulled the shawl about her, clasping it tightly. He was right. A part of her still rebelled at surrendering to any man. She could not forget what her mother had lived through for so many years. Danielle wasn't sure she could change.

"We will serve dinner soon." She hurried toward the door, needing to escape. He made her feel as though two women warred inside her for dominance.

When she shut the door on her bedchamber, she heard raised voices coming from the parlor. She welcomed the diversion as she headed toward the din. Inside the room, Gaby and Claude stood toe to toe, his face beet red, her cheeks rosy.

"You can't give her riding lessons. She's too young," Gaby shouted.

"I will do what I damned well want. Anne isn't your daughter." Claude balled his hands at his sides.

"And she isn't yours. She could get hurt."

"She needs to learn."

"She's three, you buffoon!"

"Who are you calling a buffoon?"

When Gaby fisted her hands, too, Danielle was afraid the two would come to blows. She rushed into the parlor, intending to throw herself between them. "Where is Anne? With Marte?"

For a long moment Gaby glared at Claude while he glared back.

"Gaby? Where's Anne?"

Her friend blinked and glanced at Danielle. "Why, she was right here playing with her doll." Gaby slowly turned, searching the room.

Claude walked about the parlor, his frown deepening with each step. "She was at our feet just a moment ago."

Alarm tightened about Danielle's heart. She did her own search of the area. "She's gone."

"Who's gone?" Rouen asked from the doorway.

"Anne," all three answered at once.

"How long has she been gone?"

"Only a few minutes." Claude tossed a final glare at Gaby.

"Then she can't be far away. We'll find her, Danielle." He reached out to touch her, but she stiffened.

"Rouen, I cannot wait here while you look." Panic rose in Danielle's voice as she imagined the things that might happen to Anne.

"Yes. You and Gaby must search the house while Claude and I look outside."

When the two men left, Gaby said, "This is all my fault. You left Anne with me, and if I hadn't tiffed with that man, she never would have wandered off. I'm so sorry, Danielle. I'll understand if you never speak to me again. Please forgive me."

Danielle walked into the dining room and began looking about. "Yours is not the fault. I shouldn't have been gone so long." If she hadn't been in the bedchamber admiring her husband's perfect body, Anne would still be here. She would never forgive herself if anything happened to Anne. "She is my responsibility, not yours, Gaby."

After searching every room twice, Danielle and Gaby ended up back in the parlor. Danielle paced from one end to the other, the tight coil of fear about her chest making each breath difficult. Image after image played across her mind, each worse than the one before, until she thought she would crawl out of her skin from worry.

Danielle headed for the door leading outside. "I cannot wait here. I must do something."

"I'm coming, too," Gaby said behind her.

When Danielle stepped outside, a strong wind accosted her, whipping her gown about her legs. She could smell a storm brewing as the pine trees swayed in the stiff breeze. Her alarm escalated. Anne would be so scared in a thunderstorm. Danielle wanted only to find the child so she could hold her and not let her go. Helplessness overwhelmed her as she looked about, trying to decide where to begin her search. Darkness made it impossible to see more than a few feet in front of her.

Out of the blackness that surrounded the house, Rouen rounded the corner and walked toward her, holding a lantern to guide him. "Wait inside, Danielle."

"No. Where have you looked?"

He pointed to his left. "Over there. I thought she might try to climb that oak tree again."

Claude came around the other side of the house with a lantern in his hand. "She's not by the workers' cabins. They're forming search parties to help."

The wind, its cold bite penetrating Danielle's numbness, swirled dust and leaves about the yard. She shuddered as she looked up at the moon, almost completely covered by dark storm clouds.

"Danielle, you're cold. I have no more lanterns. Go back inside. I will find her."

The gentle persuasion in Rouen's voice stiffened her resolve. She could never calmly wait for things to happen. "I will go with you."

"Very well. We'll check the stable, Claude. You and Gaby check in that direction." Rouen pointed toward the trail that led to the fort.

Danielle stared at the blackness Rouen had indicated and shivered again, this time from fear. Rouen had told her about places not far off the trail where a person could get stuck in soupy water and disappear forever. At the thought of never seeing Anne again, she had to force herself to take deep breaths of the moisture-laden air. Tears clogged her throat as she gripped Rouen's hand and followed him.

Lightning lit the clearing in front of the house

and brought Danielle to a halt. Severing her link with Rouen, she tensed, expecting thunder. There was nothing.

Rouen glanced back at her. "The storm is still far off. We'll find Anne before it hits."

Childhood memories of other storms nibbled at what composure Danielle had left. She drew in several bracing breaths and started forward. She must focus her energy on finding Anne. Nothing else mattered.

In the stable, a horse snorted as though agitated. She released Rouen's hand and hurried toward the sound. Pulling open the gate into the stall, she squinted, trying to see into the dim shadows. Rouen came up behind her and held the lantern up.

Curled on her side in the corner was Anne. Tears cascaded down Danielle's face as she scooped the child into her arms, raining kisses all over her sleepy cousin.

"Dani?"

"Yes, *ma cherie.*"

"I want to ride." Anne rubbed her eyes with her tiny fists. "Can I?"

"I think Uncle Claude has almost finished your rocking horse. Why don't you ride that first?" Tears streaked Danielle's face as she cradled the child against her, refusing to allow Rouen to take her.

"Can I ride tomorrow?" Anne yawned, closing her eyes for a moment then opening them.

"We will see, Anne."

The child wrapped her arms about Danielle's neck. "I love you." Anne laid her head on Danielle's shoulder, yawning again.

"Oh, *ma cherie,* I love you, too." Emotions swelled

in her chest, gripping her with the need to protect this little girl at all costs.

"Tell me about France," Anne murmured, her eyes sliding close.

"The houses there are huge. Our house here would be just a small part of the chateau where I grew up. And the churches have towers that reach way into the sky . . ." Danielle stared down at Anne, who had fallen asleep almost immediately. Anne threw herself into anything she did. When she finally fell asleep, it was always quickly.

"I'll take her now," Rouen said behind her.

Danielle stopped and turned toward him. "No. I'll see to her. She's my responsibility." She remembered saying those words to him on the trail after they had discovered her uncle and his burnt cabin. So much had happened since, yet it had been only six weeks ago.

"Danielle, she is *our* responsibility. When will you learn that we are partners in this marriage?"

"This partner has made the decision to return to France. Let us return on the next ship."

"No."

That word stood between them like a high stone wall impossible to scale. Danielle whirled about with Anne in her arms and marched toward the house, aware of Rouen close behind her, lighting her way.

She passed Gaby and Claude and made her way to Anne's bedchamber. The child had risen early and played hard all day. For once, Danielle was glad that Anne had taken only a brief nap earlier in front of the parlor hearth. Emotionally drained, Danielle didn't want to pretend everything was all right for

Anne's sake. She had married a stranger who lived in a strange land. Everything was not all right.

When Danielle reentered the parlor after putting Anne in her bed, the atmosphere in the room was heavy with unspoken feelings. Gaby refused to look at Claude, who was trying to ignore her. Rouen stood before the fire, frowning as he stared at the flames leaping about the logs in the hearth. Danielle eased down onto a chair before her legs gave out on her and she collapsed. She leaned her head back and closed her eyes, hoping that she never had to relive the past hour. From the moment she had picked the branches and leaves off Anne in the forest by her family's burnt cabin, Anne had become her daughter. The thought of losing her crippled Danielle with the worst fear she could imagine.

Suddenly she was as weary as Anne. All Danielle wanted to do was sleep.

"I hope you will forgive me. I should never have taken my eyes off Anne. I'll leave first thing tomorrow morning," Gaby said, her voice full of tears.

Danielle started to protest when Claude cut in. "It wasn't your fault. I started that argument. I'm to blame."

Danielle opened her eyes, intending to put an end to who was to blame for Anne's disappearance. She swallowed the words she was about to say. Claude had his arm about Gaby, who cried softly against his shoulder. He patted her back while she clutched his shirt front and soaked it with tears.

Rouen caught Danielle's attention and indicated the door. He helped her to her feet, and they left Gaby and Claude in the parlor. "They need to be alone. You look tired. I'll bring us something to eat in our bedchamber."

Danielle couldn't have resisted the suggestion if she had wanted to. At the moment, any task would require more than she had. She made her way to the bedchamber they shared and sank onto the bed, lying back on the moss-stuffed mattress. Again she closed her eyes, intending just to rest a few minutes before Rouen returned.

Rouen found Danielle asleep on the bed and placed a loaf of freshly baked bread, some cheese, and a bottle of red wine on the table nearby. He stared at his wife's face, so serene, all tension erased.

Earlier he had feared they might have lost Anne. He had been determined not to show that fear to Danielle. Now he allowed his emotions to swamp him. He had felt such helplessness while searching in the dark, unable to find Anne. When Danielle had nearly collapsed, he wanted to comfort her, to protect her, but she hadn't allowed it. As usual his wife wanted to stand by herself, facing the world alone. She still would not accept the fact they were married and Anne was now his daughter, too.

On the bed Danielle stirred, shifting her head. A tiny frown furrowed her brow. Who was she dreaming about?

Rouen pivoted away, tipped the wine bottle to his lips. He drank half the red wine and ate some bread and cheese while deciding what to do next concerning Danielle. A month before, the decision to marry had been simple. Now he realized all the complications involved in living with a woman who didn't trust easily and was resolved not to let another into her life.

He should just end his torment now—wake her and demand his husbandly rights. Looking down at her again, he reached out and touched her face with one finger, grazing the soft curve of her jaw. He wouldn't do that; he couldn't, though his body and soul needed to feel her beneath him, her essence surrounding him.

Instead, he unfastened her gown, removing layers of clothing until she was dressed only in her shift and stockings. He untied the garters about her thighs and rolled the knitted material down one leg. When he returned to take off the second stocking, he couldn't resist caressing the skin along her thigh. It felt heavenly.

He clenched his teeth, one hand clasped about the bedding while the other continued its forbidden exploration. She moaned and turned slightly into his touch. He moaned in response as he gripped the stocking and slowly inched it down her long leg, stopping to press the dimples by her knee, to cup the curve of her calf, to circle her delicate ankle.

When the stocking finally came off, Rouen bolted to his feet and backed away from the bed. Touching her was painful. He breathed in short gasps as he fought for control. How had he thought he could undress her and not become aroused? At the time, he had thought to make her comfortable. Now it would be hours before he would be.

Quickly he covered her, then headed for the parlor. He would try to sleep on the hard floor by the hearth. He came up short when he found Claude sitting in the room, staring at the fire as though he wanted to jump into it.

Rouen sat next to him. "Troubles?"

"Just one. I don't see what that woman sees in David."

"I suppose you are referring to Gaby."

"Yes. She plans to marry him."

"Has he asked?"

"Not yet."

"Then you have time."

Claude shot him a withering look. "I don't want to get married. I look at you and I don't want to go through that kind of hell. You want your wife so bad you don't know what to do."

"Marriage has nothing to do with that."

"There's no way a woman would want to sleep next to this every night." Claude indicated his scarred face.

"You have a lot to offer a woman."

Claude came to his feet. "I'm not in the market for a wife. They only complicate the situation. Good night."

Rouen watched his friend stalk off, realizing the truth in his last words. Ever since he had met Danielle, his life had not been his own. If it hadn't been for his father's meddling, he would not be wed, either. Claude was right. Danielle was definitely a complication.

ELEVEN

After putting several logs in the grate, Rouen sat in front of the hearth to warm himself. The chill of an early spring morning clung to the air. He lounged back in the chair and stared at his wife of two months. Danielle lay on her side, facing him, her features serene in sleep.

He should wake her so she could get ready to leave for the fort, but he didn't want to quite yet. He enjoyed this time each morning when he could watch her without her knowing it. She was beautiful, but what drew him was her compassionate nature. It spoke of a woman who felt deeply. Would she ever trust him completely? Rouen had asked himself that very question for the past few days as he'd fallen more and more under her spell.

A slight smile graced her full lips as she snuggled deeper into the bedding. Was she dreaming of him? Of Pierre?

During the past two months, he had courted her, getting to know her and letting her know what kind of man he was. He wanted a marriage based on friendship and mutual respect. He had known from the beginning that he would have to earn her trust after her ordeal with the Marquis.

But lately he wanted more. He leaned forward in his chair and rested his elbows on its arms, forming a steeple with his fingers. He wanted a family—not just an heir to satisfy his father, but many children. After seeing Danielle with Anne these past few months, he knew she would make a wonderful mother. Because of Danielle, Anne no longer had nightmares. She was happy and had begun to think of Danielle as her mother.

Danielle stirred again and Rouen pushed to his feet. He walked to her and knelt next to the bed. Brushing stray strands from her face, he bent to kiss her lips. He had meant it to be a light peck, but the second their mouths touched he couldn't end it. He deepened their joining as she wrapped her arms around his neck, running her fingers through his long hair. When they finally parted, a satisfied moan escaped her lips. He'd thoroughly explored them, but still couldn't look away.

"Mmm. That's an interesting way to awaken someone."

"Ma petite, you may try it with me anytime."

Danielle sat up, the covers pooling about her waist. His attention dropped to her nightgown. It didn't conceal her figure as well as he might have wished. The urge to rip the cloth from her body was so strong he moved back to the chair by the hearth before he could act on his desire—and possibly frighten her.

These past months had tested his resolve. He wanted her so; he constantly ached with need. And the worst of it was she didn't know her effect on him. Though she had lived in the Marquis's household for ten years, she didn't comprehend what went on between a man and a woman.

"Gaby must be ecstatic! She's only a few hours away from marrying Monsieur David." Danielle swung her legs to the floor and stretched, working the stiffness from her body.

Rouen made the mistake of watching her as she raised her arms high above her head and thrust out her chest while arching her back. He quickly looked away, but not before thoughts of what her body would feel like under his made him painfully aware that something in their relationship would have to change, and soon. He only had so much control. After they made love, he wouldn't be so obsessed with her. He needed to get his emotions back under his control.

He placed his hands on the mantel and leaned into it, staring at the flames devouring the firewood. "Has Gaby thought this marriage through?"

"What do you mean? Do you know something about Monsieur David?"

Rouen shook his head, not able to explain his vague feeling concerning Armand David. The man had done nothing wrong, but something wasn't quite right. Rouen had learned to trust his instincts. "I don't know much about the man. Where did he come from? He has a lot of money. How did he receive it?"

"You are a suspicious man. He told Gaby he inherited it and that he used to live in Marseilles."

"That's just his word."

"How do you know I am who I say I am? I might really be just a girl raised in a convent, not the daughter of a comte."

Rouen turned toward Danielle. "You're right. I'm sure Gaby will be in good hands."

"Gaby hasn't had much in her life, even though she was raised by nuns. She is so excited about having her own home."

"Too bad she will be so distant. You won't see her often."

"But we won't be here much longer ourselves."

"Ah, France."

"You are having second thoughts about returning to France?"

He heard the panic in her voice and smiled to reassure her. "No. But it is still almost a year from now."

"I wish we could board that ship anchored off Ship Island and sail to France today."

"I want my plantation established and running smoothly before I leave."

"Why should you care?"

"I care because I think this country is the future for France. Claude will tend the plantation for me. One of our children may wish to live here."

"I will not allow it. This place is too wild and violent."

"There is more here than that. Look at Nouvelle Orleans." Even as he spoke, Rouen knew he wouldn't change her mind about the Louisiana Colony. Danielle had a right to feel the way she did. She had seen more violence than most women.

"I prefer Paris to a city built over a swamp. It will always be provincial." Danielle walked to the chest and removed the pale green silk brocade gown she had worn to her own wedding. "I think we should agree to disagree on the subject of this colony."

Rouen strode to the door to give Danielle a chance to get dressed in privacy. With a glance back, he nearly faltered. Sunlight streamed in through the bedchamber window and showed through her nightgown, revealing her lush body. He seriously contemplated going to the bay and taking a plunge, even though the air was unusually cold and the water freezing. Something had to happen soon or he would go crazy with his desire.

Claude's frown was deeper than usual as he scanned the crowd assembled after Gaby's wedding. He spied Rouen and headed toward him. Somehow Rouen knew Claude wasn't paying a social call to Gaby and Armand, since his friend had informed him he wouldn't step near the happy couple.

"I just got word there will be a meeting between the English and the Indians allied with them in five days' time near Natchez," Claude whispered.

Rouen smelled alcohol on Claude's breath. The bottle of brandy he had given his friend had been put to good use. Claude would be the last person to admit he hated seeing Gaby marry another man.

"Who sent word?"

"Running Wolf. There's more trouble brewing. More weapons have entered the colony and he fears that won't be the end of them."

Rouen was sure his scowl matched Claude's as he turned to his friend, stepping back from the people around them. "Then we need to be there, too. Maybe the Frenchman passing on information to the English will attend. I'm curious about him, and I have a score to settle with him." He remembered the Indian raids he had witnessed and his vow to discover who was responsible for the influx of weapons to the Chickasaws.

"When do we leave?"

"First light tomorrow."

"I'll make preparations. Gives me a good reason to leave this party." Claude's attention shifted from Rouen to Gaby, who stood in the middle of a group of women.

"I'm surprised you came to give me Running Wolf's message."

"I felt it couldn't wait." Claude's frown strengthened, his eyes darkening. "She's too good for David."

Rouen forced himself not to grin. "Who is too good for David?"

"You know damned well who I'm talking about," Claude all but shouted, then strode from the room at Governor Bienville's house, uncaring of the stares that followed his exit.

"What's wrong, Rouen?" Danielle asked.

"I don't think Claude is too happy about Gaby's wedding."

"If he really cared, why didn't he speak to her?"

"He's been alone a long time, and I think he finally realizes he's lonely—especially since we will be leaving within the year. But even that wouldn't cause him to speak to Gaby about his feelings."

"What would?"

"I don't know. He thinks a woman can't love him because of his looks." Rouen shrugged. "It matters not. Gaby has wed."

"The Marquis is a very handsome man. Looks mean little."

He drew her into his embrace. "You're an unusual

woman, Danielle Beauvoir. Many women believe otherwise."

"And many men."

"True." He wanted to kiss her in front of everyone. She wore her wedding gown, and Rouen instantly remembered the vision she had made as his bride. He hardened with the suppressed desire the least bit of contact with his wife conjured up. Her lips, slightly red, beckoned him to touch them.

He forced himself to move away from her, dropping his arms to his sides. "I noticed you received a letter from France."

"I haven't read it yet, but it's from Sister Mary Catherine. She helped me to escape the Marquis. I hope she has good news to impart."

"If you want some privacy, Jean-Baptiste won't mind your using his office."

Rouen escorted her to the office and posted himself outside the door while she went into the room to read her letter from home. Twenty minutes later, she hadn't reappeared. Worried, he eased the door open and peered inside. The parchment lay on the floor at Danielle's feet. She stared at a place not far from the letter, tears slipping from her eyes.

Rouen rushed to her and knelt before her, gripping her upper arms and forcing her to look at him. "Danielle, what is wrong?"

"*Maman* died not long after I left. He killed her. Sister Mary Catherine said my mother fell down the stairs. She should have left him that night I ran away." Danielle focused on his face, blinking several times as though it were hard to see him. "I wanted her to leave him. She wouldn't. She thought he would leave me alone if she stayed. He pushed her down those stairs. I cannot doubt it."

"Have the authorities arrested him?"

"Of course not. None would dare. He's untouchable."

"No one is."

"What will I do when we return to France and I see that man again? He is evil. He will never be held accountable for my mother's death."

Rouen decided he would write his father and ask his help against the Marquis. His father had the power to see that something was done. Rouen knew what bargain to make: his father wanted his only remaining son home. Rouen would only return if the Marquis were dealt with.

Danielle wiped at her tears. "I can't let Gaby see me crying. I don't want to ruin her wedding day."

"Perhaps we should leave. The bride and groom will be going soon anyway."

She stood and picked up the letter, folding it neatly, then clutching it in her hand. "I need to speak with Gaby first."

As Danielle left the office, she tried to compose herself. She didn't want to dampen the mood for Gaby. Danielle had never seen her friend so happy, and she deserved that happiness.

Quickly Danielle found Gaby standing next to her new husband, who was talking with Pinart. When she saw Pinart, she remembered the rumor concerning how his wife had died, by falling down some stairs. Danielle made her way through the crowd, pasting a smile on her face she was afraid wouldn't last one moment. The effort it took not to pound her fists into Pinart's face held her rigid.

She pulled Gaby aside, wanting to put as much distance as she could between herself and Pinart. "I wanted to wish you well before you left." She hugged her friend. "I wish you weren't moving so far away."

"Oh, but you must come visit us as soon as we are settled. It's less than a week from here. In this vast country, that isn't far at all. Is it, Armand?" Gaby twisted about and grasped her husband's hand to draw him to her.

"No. By all means please come see us. That includes you, Pinart. We should be settled enough in a month's time to receive visitors."

"May we, Rouen?" Danielle looked expectantly at her husband, the thought of seeing her first real friend lifting her spirits, even if it meant sharing the time with Monsieur Pinart.

"If I can get away, we will." Rouen placed his hand on the small of her back.

His touch comforted Danielle. She realized of late that her husband had been her solace amidst the chaos in the colony. She felt safe for the first time in her life since her father had died, and that allowed her to take another look at her beliefs. Perhaps being married wasn't a one-sided affair. Could she put her trust in him? Could she surrender a part of herself to her husband?

Danielle kissed Gaby on both cheeks and hugged her one last time, fighting the tears that choked her throat. "*Au revoir.* Until we see each other."

Danielle made it outside to the cart before her tears fell again. She cried for her mother. She cried for the loss of her friend. Even though Gaby was just moving away, Danielle felt their relationship, forged on the ship coming to the colony, would never be the same. They would go in different directions, and that saddened her.

Rouen drew her to him, taking his handkerchief to brush the tears from her face. "I'm sorry about your mother, *ma petite.* I promise the Marquis will pay for his crime."

"How?"

"No one hurts my family. The Beauvoir name has great influence in France."

Danielle leaned back, her eyes glistening. "I loved my mother, but I lost her the day she married the Marquis. She's free now. He cannot hurt her anymore."

Rouen grazed the pad of his thumb across her cheek, his touch so soft she barely felt it. For a long moment he stared down at her, a sadness in his expression that caressed her heart and mended her pain. He drew her to him and held her while the biting wind picked up, his warmth and shelter the balm she needed.

When Rouen finally assisted her into the cart, she huddled against his side. Dark clouds were rolling in and the trees swayed. She didn't like storms. They reminded her of the Marquis, who loved them.

When they reached the house, Rouen helped her down. "Go inside and get warm. I'll see to the horse and be in soon." He looked at the blackening sky and added, "I'll have to lash everything down. This storm will be fierce."

His worried frown heightened her dread as she hurried into the house. When a storm had hit at sea, she thought they would never make it to the New World. She remembered the first time the weather had raged when she had come to live at Chateau Duchamp; the first time her mother had wept because of the Marquis.

Half an hour later, dressed for bed, Danielle stood in front of the hearth in the bedchamber, hugging her arms to her, shivering despite the warmth from the fire, the only illumination in the room. A flash of lightning followed quickly by a crack of thunder made her jump. In her mind she knew it was ridiculous to be afraid of a thunderstorm, but in her heart she couldn't stop the fear that mushroomed as the wind blew and the rain pounded the house.

Where was Rouen? He should have been inside by now. She glanced at the bedchamber door as if that would cause him suddenly to appear. It remained closed. What if something had happened to him? He could be lying unconscious in the stable.

She listened another minute to the wind and rain, then wrapped a blanket around her shoulders and headed for the door. Despite the raging weather outside, she couldn't stand around and wait, especially if there was a chance he might need her. Her hand was on the knob when it turned, and she quickly stepped back. Rouen entered, almost colliding with her.

"Where are you going?"

"Looking for you." She took in his wet appearance. His clothing was soaked, his hair plastered to his head. "You need to get out of those clothes. Here, I'll help you." She reached for his cape as he shrugged out of it.

Their hands touched. She drew back; he drew back. She lowered her gaze for a moment. When she raised her eyes again, she sucked in a deep breath. The look he sent her made her melt against him. She clutched at him for support and lifted her face to his.

She didn't care that he was wet and soaking her. She didn't care that the storm raged outside. She didn't care about anything suddenly but the man before her. For two months she had wanted him. She wanted to know what it would be like to be possessed by him, to be totally his. Above anything else tonight, she needed to feel alive, part of something wonderful.

"I need you, Rouen. Make me forget."

When his mouth came down on hers, she welcomed him, opening herself as she never thought she would. The wall about her emotions began to crumble as his tongue slipped inside to taste of her. It lay in rubble when he scooped her up in his arms and carried her to the bed, carefully placing her on the soft mattress. The feelings tumbling through her were new, the sensations overwhelming, as though fire ravaged her body.

When did I fall in love with him? For she knew she was in love as she lay before him.

He pulled back, his intent gaze capturing hers. "I want to love you, Danielle."

She untied the ribbons on her nightgown in silent answer to him. The desire in his eyes flared, making her feel womanly and wanted. When she fumbled, he took over, spreading the material to expose her breasts. He placed his palm over one, rubbing it in a circular motion. She arched into the caress, wanting more—much more.

She stilled the movement of his hand, capturing

his full attention. "I need you to make love to me now."

"I will, *ma petite.* I will."

After pushing her nightgown to her waist, he straightened and began to undress. Transfixed, she watched him strip out of his waistcoat, breeches and silk stockings. When he stood naked before her, the pool of heat in her stomach fingered outward to drown her whole body. He was magnificent, proud, as he came to her and finished taking off her nightgown. Then he stepped back and gazed down upon her, the intensity in his look sending her blood pulsating through her. She felt wanton, possessed, cherished.

Rouen stretched out beside her, one arm loosely over her. "I will take it slow and easy, Danielle, but this first time will hurt."

For a few seconds, she remembered the horrid stories Bridget had taken great pleasure in telling. Coldness edged its way into her heart. Then she thought about how kind, patient, and comforting Rouen had been these past two months. She had to trust him if their marriage was to work. She didn't want to live like her mother had.

If she loved him, it had to be totally.

One of her hands cradled his face. "I understand," she murmured, then abandoned herself to him.

His kisses rocked her to her very soul. His caresses shattered what composure she had, leaving no part of her unattended. Her body tingled with desire, attuned to his slightest movement.

Rouen levered himself up and studied her. "Are you sure, *ma petite?* This is our last chance to stop."

His soft concern flowed over her. She nodded, never taking her gaze from his face. She ran her finger across his lips, loving the feel of them, loving the man beneath them. When she trailed her hand down his chest to his flat stomach, he stiffened and drew in a sharp breath. His eyes darkened, his jaw clenched.

"I love your touch, *ma petite,* but if you continue, I can't wait for you to be ready." He lifted her hand from his stomach and placed it about his neck.

Leaning down, he sipped at her lips, then nibbled a path toward her earlobe, which he took gently between his teeth. Sensations swirled inside her, dragging her under. She was weak with needs she had never experienced, her whole body a mass of nerve endings sensitive to any change. His flesh seared hers, and he tasted of honey. The scent of him engulfed her.

She quaked when Rouen slid down her and suckled first one breast, then the other. Her nipples tightened, stoking the fire within her until it raged over every inch of her body.

His hand slipped lower, to the flesh between her thighs. She tensed. No one had ever touched her there.

He stroked her, tangling his fingers in her coarse hair, murmuring comforting words. She relaxed. When he spread her thighs apart, she welcomed him.

Deep inside, she rushed toward a cliff that looked down upon a bottomless pit. As she neared, she gave over more of herself to Rouen. He thrust a finger inside her, and she came up off the bed in mind-shattering exaltation.

Rouen settled himself over her and eased her legs farther apart. As he moved his finger in and out of her, her senses exploded and she cried out his name, her fingernails digging into his back.

"Oh, Rouen, please," she pleaded, wanting him to become a part of her.

He removed his finger, his gaze seizing hers. "Do you want me, Danielle?"

"Yes! Yes!"

He paused above her, his look still bound to hers. She became lost in the depths of his grays eyes as he positioned himself at her womanly threshold. She clung to the cliff's rim and looked into the tempting darkness, unsure what to expect.

She let go the second he drove into her. As she plunged into the abyss, pain seared her, quickly replaced by a kaleidoscope swirling with colors, sounds, and sensations.

Danielle reeled with the ecstasy of their journey. Shudder after shudder raced through her until she went limp. Rouen collapsed on top of her for a few seconds before rolling over and drawing her along his side.

Words escaped her. Exhausted, she closed her eyes and relished the night's silence. The storm had abated outside, but she had lived through her own storm and was now a woman in every sense of the word.

"I love you," she murmured, snuggling into her husband's warmth and surrendering herself to weariness.

Sunlight streamed through the window and touched Danielle's face. Smiling at her memories, she stretched and reached across the bed for Rouen. Two more times in the middle of the night he had come to her and made her soar. When she felt the empty space beside her, she opened her eyes and scanned the bedchamber. It was empty, too.

She propped herself up on her elbows, wondering where her husband was. It was later than usual for her to have awakened, but she had gotten little sleep the night before. She would dress and find Rouen. She wanted to spend the day with him. He had aroused a side of her she hadn't known existed, and she wanted to explore it further.

She hurriedly dressed and sought out Marte. The older woman was in the kitchen behind the house, baking bread. The aroma was titillating.

"Where's Rouen?"

"He had to leave. He didn't have the heart to wake you." Marte removed a loaf of bread from the oven with a wooden peel and put it on the large oak table in the center of the room.

"When will he return?" Danielle picked up Anne, who had been riding the rocking horse Claude had carved for her. As Danielle swung her around, the little girl laughed.

"He did not say." Marte averted her gaze and withdrew a piece of parchment from her apron pocket. "He left this for you."

Danielle placed Anne on the floor by the rocking horse and took the paper. The brief note stated he would be gone for several weeks—nothing about why he had left after they'd spent such a glorious night together, nothing about where he was going, nothing about how he felt, even after her own declaration of love.

She felt abandoned, alone, all her emotions evaporating as she reread the impersonal words of her husband. The warm kitchen was suddenly no longer inviting. All she could remember suddenly was that Rouen had made it plain from the very beginning he didn't want her love.

TWELVE

Rouen lay on his stomach, hidden in the brush that ringed the top of the bluff, watching the group of Chickasaws, Englishmen, and one lone Frenchman down below. He shouldn't have been surprised that Armand David was the traitor. Now that he knew, he had to decide what to do. He needed to discover if anyone else was working with David and what his plans were for the weapons coming into the colony. He strongly suspected the influx of guns was for more than the Indian raids being led by the Chickasaws.

As the group dispersed, Claude and Rouen crawled out of their hiding place and sneaked away, not saying a word until they had put some distance between themselves and the English and their allies.

But when Rouen stopped to water his horse, Claude leaped from his stallion and vented his anger. "I knew that bastard was no good for her. Let me take care of David."

Rouen knelt by the stream and cupped some water in his hands to drink. "I want to know if anyone is helping him and what they're planning to do with the weapons. Then you can have him."

"Are we going to follow him?"

"No, we're going to pay the man a visit—just like Danielle and I promised."

"I'm coming, too."

"I would have it no other way."

"Let's go, then."

Rouen chuckled. "Impatient to see a certain young woman?"

"And you aren't impatient to see your wife?"

Rouen turned away from Claude and vaulted onto his horse. Impatient wasn't quite the word he would have used. Leery and confused were better. He had left Danielle only a short note to explain why he had to leave so soon after their first true night together as husband and wife.

He had thought making love to her would end the deep ache that plagued him. It hadn't. Each day he was away from her, it intensified. He wanted her as much, if not more. He didn't like that intense need for another person.

He had watched her from the chair by the hearth as she slept that morning. He intended to wake her and tell her he had to leave, but he didn't. For the first time, he hadn't known what to say. She had told him she loved him, and he didn't know what to do about that. Their marriage had been an alliance of mutual needs. Love would only complicate their situation.

He swore he would never love another, not after watching Liliane marry his brother. He never wanted to be vulnerable like that again. He just needed time to get his emotions under control and everything would be as he planned. He and Danielle would be friends. He was her means to return to France, and she was his means to keep his father at bay and to produce heirs. It was an arrangement that would work for both of them—if he could just keep emotions out of it.

After setting the last stitch in her yellow gown, Danielle rose and shook the material. She inspected the first dress she had ever made. This was a triumphant moment, yet she didn't feel elated. Placing the gown carefully on the bed, she tried to ignore the emotions inundating her.

Rouen had been gone for over two weeks. With each day, she felt more confused, betrayed, and, yes, *angry* that the man had ridden away without a word to her.

She had given him her heart that night and he had discarded it. When she thought back to the morning after, pain made her breathing shallow. At the very least, she had needed him to hold her, reassure her that she had pleased him. He had escaped the first chance he had gotten. His actions clearly said he hadn't enjoyed making love to her. That hurt more than she cared to admit.

She folded the yellow gown and put it in her chest. Her attention strayed to Rouen's. As though her hands had a will of their own, she lifted the lid and caressed the top article of clothing, a plain white shirt that he wore when working in the fields. She brought it to her face and breathed in the clean fragrance, imagining him filling it with his muscular physique. She remembered every detail of his body from the night they had made love. An ache deep within intensified, and she quickly replaced the shirt.

Ever since her mother had married the Marquis, Danielle had known she stood alone in the world. Now that she was married, it was no different. When Rouen returned, she would make sure she protected her heart. Never again would she tell him she loved him and open herself up to greater hurt.

Slipping under the covers, Danielle relaxed on the bed, the dim light from the dying fire casting shadows about the room. Where was Rouen? Why had he left? Was her declaration so unwelcome that he needed to get away from her? Remembering how he had responded to her that night, she tried to feel more confident, but she recalled his cold note the day after and felt empty inside.

Turning her back to the door, she shut her eyes, hoping that sleep would come soon. But empty as she felt inside, the space next to her where Rouen had slept felt emptier.

The door opened and closed, and Danielle instantly tensed. She knew it was Rouen without his saying a word, sensing his presence as though he were a part of her. That unnerved her more than anything else. She wanted to stand by herself, needing no one, and somehow she would.

She listened to him move about the room, but kept her eyes closed. When he slid in beside her, she tried to relax her body as though she were sleeping.

"Danielle?"

She bit her lower lip.

He rested his hand on her shoulder. "I know you're awake. We must talk."

She shrugged off his touch and bolted upright in the bed. All her suppressed anger boiled to the surface as she rounded on him. "I have nothing to say to you, *monsieur.*"

"You are angry. I'm sorry, *ma petite.* I was gone longer than I thought."

"You could be gone until we leave for France and I would not care." She jerked the blanket up, turned her back on Rouen, and flopped onto the bed—but not before she realized he was naked. That incensed her further. Why couldn't the man sleep in a nightshirt like other men did? It was indecent!

"I know I left at a bad time, but I had a good reason."

She stiffened, squelching the hurt that threatened to swamp her.

"Claude and I are working for the Minister of Finance. We were scouting and confirming some information about the Chickasaw raids."

Danielle sucked in her cheeks and bit down on them to keep from replying. She concentrated on the pain, determined to say nothing. It was important to make him understand she didn't care about him or any secret mission he was on. She was his wife, not his friend.

He hovered behind her for a few more minutes, then lay down on his side of the bed. Soon he slept. She felt even more incensed. For the past two and a half weeks, she had tossed and turned in this large bed without him, hardly sleeping, and he came home and fell asleep instantly his first night back. Well, she would show him. She would fall asleep if it killed her.

Hours later, Danielle still hugged her side of the bed, wide awake, attuned to every move and sound that her husband made. She would get no rest this night. Her body ached in places that had nothing to do with working every waking hour to rid herself of thoughts of Rouen. But no matter how hard she worked, she couldn't forget how he had made her feel when they had made love. It had been incredible.

She whipped back the covers and rose. Dawn was hours away, but she couldn't stay in the bed another moment with Rouen. She was afraid of what she would do. And she would never let him know the power he had over her with just a simple touch. She hated her weakness, but she would learn to control it—soon, she hoped.

She sought the warmth of the hearth to chase away a chill that owed nothing to the temperature of the room. Staring down at the burning log, she tried to picture her future. Nothing materialized except a cold, lonely existence. She didn't like what she saw. It reminded her of her mother's life, and she trembled.

"Cold?"

Danielle jumped at the touch of Rouen's hand on her shoulder. Her heart pounded as she faced him and she sidestepped his touch. "Did no one teach you not to catch a person unaware?"

"Sometimes that's the best way."

She pressed her hand to her heart to slow it's beating. "You frightened me."

"Do you wish to talk now?"

"*Non.*"

He moved closer, his body pinning her to the wall beside the hearth. "You're angry with me."

"Mon Dieu, you are observant. A good quality for the minister's spy, no?"

He smiled. "Yes."

Rouen took another step closer. Danielle felt totally enveloped. She hoped she didn't show what strange things his proximity did to her insides.

"I have handled this all wrong, *ma petite.* I apologize. I should have taken my leave of you. I am unused to having a wife."

She pushed at his chest, but he didn't budge. "I accept your apology. If you'll excuse me, I have work to do."

His smile grew. "At this time of night?"

She remembered sitting up for hours sewing on her dress when she couldn't sleep while he was away. "There is no better time. No one bothers me." She stabbed him with a look that told him to back away.

He didn't. Instead, he cut the meager distance between them until his breath bathed her face. She inhaled his male scent and wished she hadn't. As usual, her pulse reacted to him, pumping blood rapidly through her body until she felt lightheaded.

"I've missed you, *ma petite.*"

"Oh?" Her voice was barely a whisper. She fought to pull air into her lungs.

"You tempt me."

She laughed shakily, heart-poundingly aware of Rouen's nakedness. "If I am so tempting, how could you leave like you did?" As she uttered the words, she wanted to take them back. Her question left her vulnerable, and she wanted, needed to be strong.

"As I told you, I had an important job. It couldn't wait." He grazed the line of her jaw with his hand. "I also needed to think."

"About what?" She leaned into his caress, her body welcoming what her mind wouldn't allow her to.

"I've never wanted a woman as I want you."

"C'est vrai? This is the truth?"

"Yes," he whispered against her lips, before taking them in a deep kiss.

His other hand caressed her face while he sought entry to her mouth, opening her up to his sweet invasion physically and mentally. As she tasted him, she wound her arms around him, drawing him so close that nothing separated them. She felt his arousal and knew he spoke the truth. He wanted her as much as she wanted him. The realization that she had pleased him their first night together emboldened her. She maneuvered him toward the bed. When he reached it, she pushed him onto the mattress and quickly stepped away from his grasp.

A frown furrowed his brow, and he started to rise.

"No," she commanded, holding up her hand.

He sank back onto the bed. Ever so slowly, she began to untie the ribbons that held her nightgown together, her gaze locked with his. When passion flamed in his eyes, scorching her with its intensity, she dropped her regard to his full lips. They were pressed together as though he could barely contain himself. Her sense of power grew.

At the sight of her husband's body sprawled on the covers, she almost didn't have the patience to finish what she had started. Danielle parted the front of her gown, exposing her breasts to him. The line of his jaw hardened as he stared at her. Slowly, she slipped the silk off her shoulders and down her arms until it pooled about her feet and she stood before him in all her feminine glory.

"Come here." He spoke through clenched teeth. "I've had enough of your games."

She remained where she was. "It is no game, Rouen. I *will* seduce you."

Before she understood his intent, he was off the bed, locking his arms about her and dragging her to him. "As I will you."

His mouth coaxed her, taking sips of her bottom lip. She flattened herself along his length, relishing the hardness that contrasted with her softness. Though her needs rendered her vulnerable, at his mercy, suddenly she didn't care. His touch destroyed her hold on sanity, and she gave in to her emotions, returning his kiss with one meant to tantalize and conquer.

Pulling slightly away, he cupped her face between his hands, capturing her full attention. "Do you know what you do to me?"

"Tell me."

His chuckle sounded deep in his throat, sexy, nerve tingling. "You make me lose control." He caressed her cheek with the back of his hand, tenderness glowing in his eyes.

She smiled slowly up at him. "Show me."

Laughter rumbled from his chest, vibrating in the air between them. He yanked her to him, his hungry mouth devouring hers, plundering what she gave gladly. She poured all her wants and needs into the joining of their lips. His hands pressed her to him until it was impossible to tell where one began and the other ended.

When he fell back on the bed, she came down on top of him, imprisoning him beneath her. She caged his hands above his head, her lips mating with his, her tongue pushing into his mouth to sweep boldly. She tugged at his earlobe, then trailed a path down his neck to his chest where she toyed with his nipples, sucking first on one, then the other.

With a swiftness that took her breath away, she was on her back and he was on top of her. As she stared up at her husband, Rouen was no longer the gentleman. He was every inch a man comfortable in the wilderness, living off the land, fighting for what was his. The thought that he was so capable of defending her sent her heart speeding out of control. She squeezed her eyes closed to still the spinning world.

His lips followed the same path as hers, first sampling her mouth, then teasing her earlobe before he turned his attention to her breasts. Sensation after sensation bombarded her, making her conscious of his every movement.

When he opened her legs to settle himself between her thighs, her body was a mass of nerve endings sensitive to the slightest touch, smell, taste. When he entered her, she arched into him, wanting skin against skin, lips against lips. When he drove deeper and deeper, her climax overwhelmed her, explosions of pleasure ripping through her. She cried out his name as she collapsed back on the bed.

He came down and gathered her into his arms,

rolling over onto his back while she nestled at his side. "That, *madame,* is what happens when I lose control."

"Mmm. I like that."

"We must talk."

His voice lulled her into a sense of contentment. The edges of sleep crept closer. "Later," she managed to mumble before darkness enveloped her.

Sunlight poured through the small window, warming Danielle's face. She snuggled deeper into the mattress and reached for Rouen. The bed was empty. She sat up and looked around the room. He was gone. Throwing back the covers, she rose, trying not to feel abandoned, betrayed again. She couldn't keep her hands from shaking, however, as she donned her gown.

He had said they must talk. What if he had wanted to tell her he had to leave again? What if he had only come home for one night and was off on another mission? She needed him here. She needed reassurance that what she experienced when they made love was real.

She halted inside the parlor doorway. Rouen was on his hands and knees with Anne riding on his back. Danielle couldn't contain her laughter when he made sounds like a horse, rearing up and trying to buck Anne from him. Holding onto his neck, Anne glanced up at Danielle and giggled. She slid off Rouen's back and hurried to Danielle, hugging her about the legs.

"*Papa*'s home. *Papa*'s home."

Danielle looked at Rouen, who was smiling like a man who had just become a new father. And in a sense that was the case. Anne had never called him *papa* before now. Danielle's throat tightened with emotions she would have to sort out later when she could deal with this added dimension to their family. Tears filled Danielle's eyes.

"Maman, is something wrong?"

Anne had given her the most precious gift she could. This was the first time she had called her *maman.* She picked up the child and kissed her plump cheek. "Oh, no, Anne. Everything is wonderful. Have you been having fun riding the horsie?"

"Papa is a great horsie. But one day I'll have my own. *Papa* said so."

"He did?" Danielle stared at Rouen.

"I told her about a gentle horse at Chateau Beauvoir that would be perfect for her. When I left, Morning Mist was only two years old. She was the only horse that tolerated small children."

"I'm not small, *Papa.* Claude says I'm big."

Rouen took Anne from Danielle and hoisted her up on his shoulders. "Now you're big."

Anne's giggles saturated the house with warmth as Rouen carried her into the dining room, pretending she was going to bump her head on the door frame because she was so big. Danielle followed, feeling for the first time that the future looked bright. Anne had accepted them as her parents. They would be returning to France soon. And making love to Rouen was unbelievable.

"No, I'm not going to tell her why we're going to Gaby's." Rouen downed the contents of his wineglass in one swallow.

"Maybe you should." Claude stood by the mantel in the parlor, jabbing at the fire with an iron poker.

"And what if Danielle says something to alert David? That would put everyone in jeopardy, especially her. I can't risk that."

"She might be able to help us. She could talk to Gaby about what David is doing."

"No, I don't want her in more danger than she will be just by visiting his plantation. If I could go without Danielle, I would. But her absence would alert David that something was wrong."

"It might be best if I scout the area without anyone knowing I'm there. I'll follow you two and camp out in the woods."

"Wouldn't it be better if both of us work on David?"

"No." Claude's denial spoke of a man torn by emotions he wished he didn't feel.

Rouen wanted to help Claude, but he couldn't. "I'm sorry Gaby married David. But it does give us a reason to visit him."

"She's going to get hurt no matter what. She'll be caught in the middle. Her husband's a traitor to his country."

"And not good enough for her."

"You're damned right!" Claude pounded his fist against the mantel.

"What will you do when she's free?" Rouen had promised himself that he would take care of the traitor responsible for the raids on the settlers. He would never forget that man's screams as he slowly died. Even now, he broke out in a cold sweat thinking about his trip with Danielle into the wilderness.

"Do?" Claude's eyebrows rose as though he hadn't thought about Gaby being free in the future.

"She will need someone. She can't live in the colony alone."

"There's nothing for me to do. She doesn't like me."

"Do you like her?"

"She's pigheaded and much too independent for me."

"Do you like her?"

Claude faced Rouen, his eyes bleak. "Yes. I could never live with a woman who couldn't stand up to me and speak her mind. Gaby does. But I'm not the kind of man she wants. David is."

"Women have a way of changing their minds."

"Speaking from experience?"

Rouen saw the twinkle enter his friend's eyes and was glad he could wipe that look of desolation from Claude's face. "I've probably had considerably more experience with women than you, *mon ami*. After all, you've been in the colony a lot longer than I have."

"Does your wife know about that experience?"

"She knows I was married in France."

"And Liliane?"

"She knows about her, too. There are no secrets between us."

"You're forgetting the real reason we're going to see the Davids."

"That's for her protection. I won't let anything happen to Danielle."

"You speak like a man in love."

Rouen remembered the night before, spent making love to his wife. "Danielle and I are well suited.

Love has nothing to do with it. We'd better start planning our trip."

Claude's regard slid from Rouen to a place behind him. Rouen turned and saw Danielle standing in the parlor doorway. Her cheeks were white, her eyes bright. She blinked, as though mentally shaking herself, and plastered a smile on her face.

"Anne finally went to sleep even though she wanted to stay up and be with her *papa.*" Danielle clasped her trembling hands and made her way to the chair opposite Rouen. "What trip are you talking about?" she asked, realizing the men were waiting for her to say something while what she wanted was to flee and console herself.

"The trip to see Gaby."

Danielle knew she should be excited about seeing her friend, but all she remembered at the moment were her husband's words. *Love has nothing to do with it.* To her, love had everything to do with their marriage. No matter how hard she tried, she couldn't change how she felt about Rouen. She loved him. He didn't love her. It was that simple. It was that devastating. The bright future she envisioned dimmed.

"You want to see Gaby, don't you?" Rouen frowned.

Danielle realized she was expected to comment on the trip. "Of course. I miss her. Will you join us, Claude?"

"No. There's too much to do here." Claude glanced toward the fire, picking up the poker to shift the logs around.

"Gaby will be disappointed."

Claude pivoted toward Danielle. "Why do you say that?"

"She enjoys your *repartee.* It's a shame you weren't bolder, Claude. For a man who once wrestled a bear, you are timid when it comes to women."

Claude reddened. "You and Gaby talked about me?"

"Why, *monsieur,* I do not break confidences." Secretly she felt Claude was better for Gaby than the man she married, but it was too late now. To ease Claude's obvious distress, Danielle asked, "What must I do to prepare for our trip?"

"You need only pack your personal items and clothing."

"How long will we be away?" She needed to focus on something other than her ache over Rouen's statement to Claude about their marriage.

"I do not know."

"Then Anne will come with us?"

"No!"

Danielle stared at her husband, confused by his adamant reply. "But I do not wish to be long away from her, now that she accepts us as her parents."

"Danielle, do you remember the last trip we made into the wilderness?"

She sucked in a deep breath, the images flashing through her mind. "Perhaps we shouldn't go."

"I have business with David. It should be safe enough, but I will take no unnecessary risks with Anne."

"What kind of business?"

"Nothing you need worry about." Rouen stood. "Now, if you'll excuse us, Claude and I must check on a mare that's ready to foal."

Danielle watched her husband leave, irate at his dismissive reply to her question. Partners indeed! His idea of partnership differed from hers. She might not have her husband's love, but she would command his respect. He was not going to coddle her as though she were incapable of taking care of herself. Rouen had a few lessons to learn about his well-suited wife.

THIRTEEN

Gaby ran down the steps and threw herself into Danielle's outstretched arms. "I have counted the days until this moment." Tears flowed as they hugged.

Danielle pulled back and looked into Gaby's face, noting the faint circles under her friend's eyes and her too-pale skin. "You are all right, *non?*"

"I'm fine. It is the move and the excitement of this grand house. I never believed I would become the mistress of this." Gaby indicated the two-story red brick house.

"Where's Armand?"

"He's inside. Rouen, I am to tell you he had some business he needed to finish, but he will meet you before dinner in the grand salon. He has a bottle of brandy that he thinks you might like to sample."

Something was wrong with Gaby. None of her usual gaiety was evident in her voice. It worried Danielle. She hoped it was excitement, as her friend had said, but during the journey, she had tried to dismiss a sense of foreboding. "Are you sure you want visitors so soon after your marriage?"

"Oh, yes. You are always welcome in my home." Gaby swept her arm toward the large front door.

"Please come in. We shall talk and rest until dinner. You must be tired after your journey."

Danielle and Gaby mounted the steps while Rouen took the horses to the stable, insisting on seeing to his animals himself.

Inside, Danielle stopped and gazed at the beauty before her, stunned by it in the midst of the primitive colony. Rows of doors ran down both sides of the large entrance hall. A winding staircase led to the second story. The polished wood reflected the sun. Indeed, Armand David was richer than she or Rouen had thought.

"How beautiful, Gaby."

"Yes, I was surprised. I never expected to be a mistress of such a place. But Armand wanted something to remind him of France."

Danielle slanted a look at her friend. Gaby should have been elated that her dream had come true, but nothing in her expression or tone of voice indicated that. Again Danielle felt uneasy.

"I'll show you to your bedchamber."

When her friend opened the door to the room she and Rouen were to share, Danielle's breath caught. She stared at the tester covered in a bedspread of gold and green embroidered silk with a matching canopy. Heavy green velvet draperies had been pulled back with gold braided ropes to allow in the sun. The high sheen of the wood downstairs was echoed in the furniture in the bedchamber.

"How long will you be able to stay?" Gaby asked as a slave entered the room and placed two bags on the floor. She waved the young black girl away, saying, "I will assist Madame Beauvoir."

Danielle walked to the window and stared out at

the forest a few hundred feet away. She felt as if someone was watching the house, and a shiver of apprehension slithered up her spine. Clasping her arms to her, she swung about to face her friend. "Only a few days. Besides having some business with your husband, Rouen has some with another person in the area."

The smile on Gaby's face fell for a brief moment. "You can't stay longer?"

"No. Rouen doesn't care to be too long from his plantation. There is much to do in the springtime. I'm surprised we came now. He worked so hard before your wedding to prepare his fields for planting."

Everything about this trip seemed strange to Danielle. She couldn't decide why, but the feeling wouldn't leave her. With Gaby's unusual behavior, the uncomfortable feeling was intensifying.

"Well, I am glad for your visit. The only people around for miles are the slaves. Armand doesn't want me to become too friendly with them. I've never owned anyone before. I'm most uncomfortable with the situation," Gaby said in a lowered tone. "How is everyone? Anne? Marte? Sister Gertrude?" Her pause was almost imperceptible. "Claude?"

"They're fine. I thought Claude would come with us, but he didn't."

"Is he still as gruff as ever?"

"Claude is Claude. Since he and Rouen returned from hunting a week ago, he has been most silent, always scowling." She had almost told Gaby about the two men working for the Minister of Finance, but Rouen had made it clear no one should know.

"That's Claude's usual demeanor," Gaby said in an almost wistful tone as she stared out the window.

"How is married life?"

Gaby looked back at Danielle, her expression neutral. "I could ask you that question. Even when I was at the fort, you were quiet on that subject."

"Rouen and I have an understanding," Danielle said, remembering his declaration to Claude about love not being a part of their marriage. Since that evening, he had been aloof toward her except when he came to her at night. She didn't want to love him, but she did. The knowledge saddened her. Love wasn't a part of their agreement. It complicated everything between them, according to Rouen. She saw only heartache in her future. She wanted so much more than what they had originally agreed to when they had married.

"Do you love your husband?" Gaby stood and paced the bedchamber, her actions restless.

She had said it once out loud to Rouen, and he had made it clear he didn't want to hear it. She wouldn't say it out loud again, not even to Gaby. "I could ask you that question."

"No." Gaby stopped in the middle of the room and glanced about her as if she were checking to make sure no one was eavesdropping.

"What troubles you, Gaby? Do not deny it, my friend. I know you."

All pretenses evaporated as her friend collapsed in a chair and tears shone in her eyes. "He isn't what he seems. He's—mean. No. Evil is a better word."

"Oh, Gaby." Danielle was instantly at her side, hugging her. Danielle knew what her friend must be going through. She had watched her mother live with an evil person for ten years. "You shall come back to Riverview with us."

"No! Impossible! I am his wife."

"We must do something. I can't leave you here with that man." She would never leave anyone at the mercy of a cruel man again. Her mother died because of the Marquis. She wouldn't allow the same thing to happen to Gaby. "Let me talk with Rouen. He will know what to do."

"Danielle, if Armand finds out you know, he will beat me again."

"He beat you!"

"Several times. It is a husband's right, but I don't know if I can go through—" Gaby swallowed hard, trying to find the words. Instead, tears streamed down her face.

Danielle's heart ached. Rouen might not love her, but he never mistreated her. She would save Gaby somehow. She had left her mother with the Marquis and he had killed her. She would never forgive herself for that. Gaby would not suffer her mother's fate. "I'm surprised your husband allowed us to visit."

"At our wedding it was his idea to ask you."

Danielle frowned, puzzled over the reasoning behind Armand's invitation. Again she shivered, even though the afternoon was unseasonably warm.

When Rouen entered the bedchamber, Gaby turned away, swiped at her face, then excused herself without looking at him. Danielle waited until the door was closed before saying anything.

"We have to help Gaby escape Armand. He's beating her."

Rouen shrugged out of his coat. "She's married to him. We can do nothing. Do not meddle, Danielle."

"But, Rouen—"

He strode to her and clasped her arms, drawing her close. "I am your husband, *madame.* You will do as I say."

Fury gripped her at his audacity. She actually wanted to do physical harm in that moment. She clenched her hands so tightly that her fingernails dug into her palms. "The Marquis killed my mother. I will not stand by and watch another woman I care about be killed by a man."

"Then we will leave tomorrow. I will not have you put in danger because you want to interfere between a husband and wife." His stormy look chilled her. His fingers bit into her arms, bespeaking of his reined-in anger.

"Take your hands from me. I will do nothing to interfere."

"You must promise me, Danielle."

She nodded, realizing she was lying to her husband. He had given her no choice in the matter. She would protect her friend whether he wanted her to or not.

Rouen quickly changed from his riding clothes into a full-cut coat, a waistcoat, and breeches for dinner. "I will be with David in the parlor. Don't keep us waiting too long."

When he left, Danielle sank down onto the chair, shaking with her anger at both Armand and Rouen. She had fallen in love with a man who had no honor. How could Rouen let that monster beat Gaby? How could she be so wrong about the man she married—the man she loved?

Danielle couldn't hold back her tears. Love wasn't possible for her. She had been right when she had come to this colony. She could only depend on herself. Emotions made a person weak, vulnerable.

Lying perfectly still, Danielle clung to her side of the bed, her back to Rouen. She couldn't sleep. All she could think about was the evening she had just spent with Armand David, who played the charming host as though he didn't beat his wife and everything was as it should be. Her stomach was still tied in knots, the tension as much a part of her as her next breath. She had hardly touched the painstakingly prepared roasted pig.

Rouen slid from the bed and dressed. Danielle opened her mouth to speak, but stayed her words when he made his way to the window. She turned slightly to watch him as he slipped out of the opening and disappeared from her view.

Frowning, she moved to the window, peering into the darkness. Rouen raced across the yard and met someone at the edge of the forest.

What was going on? Why had Rouen sneaked out of the house? Who was he meeting?

She started to turn away when she saw Armand leave the house. She would know that man's swaggering walk anywhere. He headed for the slave quarters. This was her chance to talk with Gaby and see if she could get her friend to leave with her.

With only the moonlight to guide her she, too, dressed, then quickly made her way to the bedchamber Gaby shared with Armand. Danielle opened the door without knocking and entered, searching for her friend in the darkness. The dying fire in the hearth illuminated the room, and Danielle saw Gaby on the bed, curled into a tight ball. Her friend's sobbing filled her with dread.

She hurried to Gaby. "What's wrong? Has he hurt you?"

Gaby stiffened, then struggled to a sitting position, brushing at her face. "You shouldn't be in here. He might come back any minute."

Danielle found the candle on the bedside table and lit it, gasping when she saw bruises on her friend's arms. They had been covered by her gown earlier. "You're coming with me now. I won't let you stay another night with that man. Rouen can catch up with us later, if he cares to." She remembered her husband's earlier command that she not interfere with Gaby's marriage. He expected her to obey him because she was his wife. He would quickly learn that would never be a reason she would do as he said.

"No. Armand won't let me go. I won't put you in danger."

Danielle felt as though she had slipped back in time. Once she had begged her mother to leave the Marquis. Her mother had wanted to protect her. There was no way Danielle would allow history to repeat itself.

"That's why I won't leave you. No one has the right to beat another, not even a husband." Rage caused her words to come out in a harsh whisper that spoke of her determination. Gaby was the one who needed protection, not her. "I won't leave this room without you."

She would never abandon someone in trouble ever again, even if she had to kidnap her friend for her own good. "Please, Gaby, I can't leave you behind."

Slowly Gaby crawled from the bed and limped toward the wardrobe. "He'll come after us. He values his possessions. No one takes what is his."

"I won't let him hurt you again." Danielle knew what would happen if she left her friend behind. She would die. Perhaps not right away, but sometime in the future Armand David would go too far, hit her one too many times, and kill her.

Gaby removed her nightgown, and Danielle's anger escalated when she saw the bruises that marked her friend's back, chest, and legs. "How many times has he hit you?"

Gaby stared down at her body, tears welling in her eyes. "Too many, especially this past week, ever since he returned from his trip. It's not just me, either. He beats the slaves at the least provocation. Everyone is frightened of him."

"Get dressed. I've got to get something from my room, then we will be gone."

Danielle rushed back to her bedchamber and rummaged through Rouen's bag until she found one of the loaded pistols he carried. If Armand came near them, she would kill him before she would let him take her friend away. It was the least she could do in memory of her mother. She hid the pistol in the inside pocket of her cloak.

She met Gaby and silently took her hand to lead her to the stable. The candle Danielle held to light their way flickered in the gentle breeze. Pine and spring perfumed the air. A chorus of insects sounded in the stillness, proclaiming to the world that life went on.

Her friend's reluctance grew with each step away from the house. Gaby shook as though at any second Armand would leap from the blackness and whisk her away. Danielle's pulse sped as she scanned the curtain of night that surrounded them.

She wouldn't think about that possibility. If the truth were known, she hadn't thought beyond getting away from the house. When they reached the stable, she slowed her pace and crept up to the building, alert for Armand, but the place was deserted except for several horses in their stalls.

"You saddle a horse while I saddle my mare," Danielle whispered close to Gaby's ear with a bravado she didn't feel. She didn't want her friend to know how scared she was.

Gaby nodded and followed her inside. Danielle went to the stall that held her mare and saddled the animal. With each passing second, she felt more confident everything would work out. Her heart slowed its rapid tempo.

Danielle led her horse over to the stepping block to mount her. Plans for what they would do once they were away from the house formed in her mind. She remembered the path she and Rouen had taken to the plantation. She had a good sense of direction, and she was sure she could find it even in the moonlight. It was on the other side of the house, a wide gap in the line of trees.

She started to vault into the saddle when she noticed that Gaby stood by an unsaddled horse. She held the reins and stared at a point by the horse's shoulder.

"Gaby?"

"I don't know how to saddle a horse. Until I came

here, I'd never ridden a horse. That was what made Armand so mad at me in the beginning. I caused our trip here to be longer than usual. He wasn't happy."

"Me, I care little what makes him happy."

"Where in hell do you two think you're going?"

Danielle froze at the sound of Armand's voice. She made a move for the pistol, but two arms locked about her and yanked her back against a huge, hard body. Her captor swung her around.

Armand had gripped Gaby's arm so hard she winced and leaned into him, tears of pain in her eyes. "My, my," he said, "what do you have inside that cloak?"

Armand nodded to her captor, and he shifted, gripping her with only one arm while he searched her. He discovered the pistol and presented it to Armand.

Armand advanced on Danielle, dragging Gaby behind him. With one jerk, he removed Danielle's cloak. He examined the rest of the garment, then tossed it to the side.

"We can't have any more little surprises, can we?" Armand tucked the pistol into his breeches. "Search her."

Danielle twisted and thrashed as the huge man who held her began to run his hands down her body, fondling her in places where no weapon could possibly be hidden. She tried to scream, but Armand slammed the back of his hand across her face. Pain exploded in her jaw, and she tasted her own blood.

"Say one word, *madame*, and I will take my frustration out on Gaby." Armand yanked his wife in front of him and locked his arm around her neck, tightening his hold until she began to choke.

"She has no more weapons," the other man said in an English accent.

"Take them to the cabin. We will deal with them there in privacy."

"And her husband?"

"I would lay a trap for him, but now my plans must change. Everything must be advanced. We will dispose of him tonight. I'll see to that. You watch them."

"No!" Danielle said without thinking.

Armand pressed his arm into Gaby's throat. Her face reddened and terror filled her eyes. "Have a care for your friend, *madame.*"

"Please." Danielle fought the tears that threatened. This man would take pleasure in her misery, just like the Marquis.

"Please what? Spare your husband? Spare you? Or spare my dear wife, of whom I tire quickly?" He eased his hold on Gaby. "I can't say I won't enjoy what I'm about to do." He swung his wife around and struck her in the jaw.

Before Danielle could react, Armand pivoted and drove his fist into her face. Blackness mingling with pain swept her away as she sank to the ground.

The instant Rouen stepped into the clearing, Claude was awake with a pistol trained on him.

"You haven't lost your touch."

"You know better than to sneak up on me. Why are you back?"

"When I went to the house, I found Danielle missing. I fear she has done something foolish. Her mare is gone. Gaby is gone, too. Danielle told me she wouldn't allow Gaby to stay with a man like Armand."

Claude muttered a few choice words as he rose. "Women. We'll track them. Then you can straighten your wife out."

"That's just it. There is more than one set of horses leaving the stable. We need to split up."

Rouen hoped it was just Danielle disobeying him, not something else. But as he followed the tracks of two horses that led into the dense pine forest, periodically dismounting to check the ground, he couldn't rid himself of the feeling that something was terribly wrong. His gut knotted with tension, his neck and shoulders stiff.

He should have realized Danielle wouldn't listen to him. A woman of such passion would never sit idly by and watch a friend be hurt. Claude was right. He should have told her he was here to catch a traitor. But he had been so concerned that she would give them away to David. For years he had trusted few people. Now it might cost him his wife. The knot in his gut hardened into a fist.

As he slowly, painstakingly made his way through the forest, alert for any sign of Danielle or Gaby, he realized his wife had come to mean much to him. Denying his feelings would not change that. After he made sure she was all right, he was going to wring her neck, then kiss her thoroughly and never let her go.

The darkness faded as consciousness weaved its way through Danielle's mind. She came awake but kept her eyes closed. The scent of old wood and dirt filled her nostrils, and the feel of coarse wool was beneath her. Her jaw throbbed, a constant reminder of what Armand and the Englishman were capable of.

Someone stirred, and she slowly opened one eye halfway. Gaby lay on a cot across the cabin while the huge Englishman stood in front of the hearth, staring down at a cold fireplace. When Danielle moved slightly, the hemp that bound her hands chafed her wrists.

She stamped down the panic that mushroomed inside of her. Her heart beat at triple its usual rate. She had to remain in control or she wouldn't be able to figure a way out of this mess.

She couldn't count on Rouen to save her. He had gone earlier—she didn't know where—and he certainly wouldn't know where she was when he finally returned to the house. If he returned. Armand and the Englishman had threatened Rouen's life. Why were they after her husband?

Rouen must be up to something. He had warned her not to interfere. Even knowing the outcome, Danielle would do it all over again. She could never leave Gaby alone with that monster, and Rouen had given her no choice in the matter.

If Rouen had come to the plantation because he worked for the Minister of Finance and Armand was doing something wrong, then why hadn't he told her what was going on? He'd had plenty of opportunities. Anger, directed at her husband, made her grit her teeth. A sharp pain streaked down her neck, forcing her to relax her tense jaw.

The Englishman turned from the hearth. Danielle closed her eyes and pretended she was still unconscious. She heard his footsteps approaching her, and it took all her willpower not to become stiff. After he checked her tied wrists, she sensed him kneeling next to her cot. Suddenly she felt his hand on her face and reacted by flinching.

"Ah, I see you have decided to wake up."

Danielle slowly opened her eyes. His leer greeted her, and she recoiled as far from him as possible on the narrow bed.

He reached out to her again, running his finger down her jaw where she was sure it was swollen and red. "He is a bit rough. If you're nice to me, I can be a lot gentler."

She gritted her teeth to keep from speaking her mind and further enraging the man hovering over her. Again pain shot through her jaw and down her neck, but she didn't reply.

"He will return soon. Then we'll see if you remain quiet. I always did fancy a Frenchy."

As his hand trailed down her throat to her breast, Danielle twisted away and turned her back on the Englishman, plastering herself as much as possible against the rough cabin wall. He laughed. The sound reverberated through her mind with his intention. She redoubled her efforts to keep her panic from taking over and sent a silent prayer to Rouen to find her. Otherwise, she didn't know how she would get out of this predicament. After her husband rescued her, she'd give him a piece of her mind for not trusting her.

When the Englishman stepped outside the cabin, Danielle whispered, "Gaby, are you awake?"

"Oui. I heard what that man said. Danielle, what are we going to do?"

"I don't know. Let me think." Her thoughts swirled with possibilities, but Danielle couldn't seem to think of one that would work. "Maybe I could appeal to his humanity."

"Are you daft?"

"Then how about his masculinity?"

"That might work. He is taken with you."

"Pretend you are unconscious—no matter what," Danielle whispered as someone approached the cabin door.

Hope blossomed within her that something had happened to the Englishman and she would be rescued—even if her rescuer was Rouen, who right now wasn't in her good graces. But when the door swung open, the Englishman stood in the entrance. His gaze immediately sought hers. She trembled.

"Where have you been?" Danielle asked, surprised that her voice worked when her throat was tight and her pulse hammered so hard that she was sure he could hear it.

"Relieving myself." His smile frosted her. "Didn't think a woman of your genteel breeding would want to see that. I see you've had a change of mind. No more silent treatment?"

"What good would it do? My fate is in your hands."

He covered the distance in two strides and sat on the cot, pushing her against the wall. "Right you are. You're a sensible chit."

"I am that. Perhaps we will make a bargain before Armand returns, *non?*"

He scowled. "What kind of bargain?"

"I know things to make your blood boil, *monsieur.* Life at the French court is quite risque. Perhaps you have heard? Would you like me to show you a few of the things I've learned?" Danielle hoped her smile would stay in place long enough to convince this man, since she had never been to court and certainly didn't know any tricks. "Me, I can bring a man to ecstasy with my fingers." What she wanted to do was get them around his neck and squeeze.

Sweat popped out on his forehead as he stared down at her. He swallowed visibly, his gaze darting to Gaby, lying on her cot perfectly still. He rose. "Show me."

Danielle raised her hands. *"C'est difficile.* They are bound together."

"If you think to trick me, it won't work."

"Me? You outweigh me by ten stone and you are a foot taller. How could I trick such a big, strong man?" she mocked, steeling herself for his wrath.

He tossed back his head and laughed. "You're right. I could kill you with one hand." He bent and untied the rope about her wrists.

Danielle rubbed her raw skin and savored the brief moment of freedom until the Englishman hauled her to her feet and pressed her against his arousal.

"Show me what you do with those hands." Shoving her back, he unfastened his breeches and dropped them to the ground.

Danielle's heart stopped. What had she done? She knew only what Rouen had taught her. She stared at a spot on the Englishman's shoulder to avoid looking down and moved a step closer to him. Her hands quaked as she reached for his drawers. She could do this. She had no choice until she came up with a way to disable him.

Suddenly Gaby screamed and jumped on the man's back, bringing her bound hands over his head to put a lock about his neck. Danielle was almost as surprised as the Englishman, who whirled about trying to dislodge her friend.

Danielle searched the cabin for a weapon. Her gaze fell upon a stool in front of the hearth. She hurried to it and picked it up. Without another thought, she swung it down on the man's head. His eyes popped open like two round saucers. He staggered forward and fell, with Gaby still holding on. The air swooshed from her friend's lungs, and she collapsed against the Englishman's back.

"Are you all right?" Danielle quickly untied Gaby's hands and helped her to stand.

" 'Tis a good thing I saw that coming and got out of the way. I was about to bite the man's ear."

"Come, we must leave."

"Oui."

Danielle and Gaby raced for the door. Danielle thrust it open and hurried into the predawn. When she heard voices coming toward the cabin, she came to a halt, looked frantically around, then dove for the thick underbrush, pulling Gaby along behind her. Peering out of the branches, she tensed. Armand approached them, his pistol trained on Claude.

"You can join the others until I have found Beauvoir. Then I'll let the Indians deal with you two while I entertain the women. Much more amusing."

The hideous cackle that followed Armand's declaration iced Danielle's spine. What should she do? She needed help, but there was no time to get it.

Her hand closed over a rock near her foot and divine inspiration struck.

Inhaling a deep breath, she rose, aimed, and hurled the rock at Armand's pistol hand. The weapon flew from his grasp, and a curse exploded from his lips. He and Claude pounced for the gun.

Danielle whirled, searching for something to use against Armand if he won the battle for the pistol. Her gaze riveted on Rouen, who lounged against a tree, his gun cradled in the crook of his arm, patiently awaiting the outcome. He scowled at her, then returned his attention to the pair wrestling for the gun.

"Your husband, he is not pleased," Gaby whispered.

"Nor am I pleased with him."

"I wonder how long he has been there."

"I do not know." Danielle didn't want to think about the consequences she faced if he had seen her hurl the rock at Armand. She had done what she had to; he would say she had put herself needlessly in danger. None of this would have happened if he had told what was going on. She would inform him of that just as soon as he had taken care of Armand.

Claude raised himself up and smashed his fist into Armand's face. The sound echoed in the small clearing, and Danielle barely resisted the urge to applaud. The man deserved far worse, but at least he was not moving.

Claude grabbed the pistol and leaped to his feet. He cocked a grin at Rouen. "What took you so long?"

"I've been here the whole time. I was just waiting

for the right moment. I didn't want to shoot the wrong man." Rouen flicked Danielle a withering look. "Of course, I didn't know my wife was going to take matters into her own hands."

"What do you want to do with him?"

"Let's tie him up in the cabin before he regains consciousness. I have a few questions to ask him before turning him over to the authorities at Fort Rosalie."

"Excuse me, Rouen," Danielle said, upset that her voice squeaked. She had the right to be angry, not him.

He arched a brow. "Yes?"

"There's another man in the cabin you will need to tie up, too."

"What happened to him?"

"I hit him with a stool."

The corner of his lips twitched with a smile. "Well, I must say you are resourceful."

Danielle came out from behind the bush. "Thank you," she replied in a voice she hoped bespoke her reined-in anger.

Rouen came to her and pulled a twig from her hair. "I will speak with you after I've dealt with these men. You and Gaby go back to the house and wait for me." The steel thread in his voice warned her to do exactly as he commanded, though she was tempted to defy him. "It is safe?"

"If it isn't, I trust you will defend yourself. But take this—just in case." He thrust Armand's pistol into her hand. "Remain there, Danielle."

She felt his gaze on her as she strode away from the cabin. He was definitely not happy with her. Then she remembered why she had taken such a risk. Rouen had refused to help Gaby. Her anger built again. He had some explaining to do himself.

At the clearing's edge, she turned back to see what was keeping Gaby. Her friend came out from behind the bush and approached Claude, her gaze darting to Armand lying on the ground.

"Are you all right, Claude? Did you hurt yourself?" Gaby took Claude's hand in hers and examined it.

The most tender look Danielle had ever seen crossed Claude's face as he stood with Gaby and told her he was fine. In that moment, Danielle knew Gaby's future would be with Claude. It might take the man a while to realize it, but he loved her and she loved him.

Rouen watched Danielle leave, fighting the strong urge to call her back, pull her into his arms, and run his hands all over her body to make sure she was indeed all right. From the moment she had risen up out of the bush and thrown the rock at David, his emotions had ranged from relief she was alive to fury that she had placed herself in such danger. First he would see to Armand David and the man in the cabin so they would no longer be a threat to his family. Then he would see to his wife.

He helped Claude drag David inside, tying him up while Claude saw to the man Rouen recognized as one of the Englishmen with the Chickasaw raiding party. The man's breeches lay about his feet.

"When this one comes to, I have a few personal questions for him." Claude pulled the hemp tight around the man's wrists. "If he wasn't still clad in his drawers, he would be a dead man."

"You would have had to wait your turn."

Rouen looped the rope about David's ankles. He had difficulty containing his anger. He wanted to treat David to the same torture the settlers had suffered. But first he needed some answers. Then he would turn David over to the French authorities at the fort, where the man most assuredly would be shot for treason.

After the two men were restrained, Rouen sat on the cot to wait until David regained consciousness. Judging by the pieces of rope and the messy cots, Danielle and Gaby had been held captive in the cabin. His blood churned when he thought about what they might have gone through. David and the Englishman might not make it to the fort to stand trial after all.

"I shouldn't have hit him so hard. We may be here for a while."

Rouen's scowl deepened. The urge to do bodily harm to David was so strong that he couldn't force himself to relax the rigid set of his body. "You should have hit him harder."

David groaned and tried to get up, but his hands and feet were bound. His gaze shot to Rouen's. "What's the meaning of this?"

"I'm the one who will ask the questions." Rouen squatted next to David, barely containing his anger. "Are you expecting another shipment of weapons?"

David blinked, his face red with indignation. "What are you talking about? Wait till the authorities learn of your actions."

"Oh, they will learn of this." Rouen unsheathed his knife and ran the point down the man's cheek, coaxing a thin line of blood to the surface. "Where are the weapons? I overheard you talking to the Englishmen and the Chickasaws about new ones arriving soon. When? How are they coming into the colony?"

David's eyes widened as Rouen's blade continued to draw a trail of blood down his neck, stopping at his collarbone. Though fear shone in David's gaze, he remained silent.

"In my dealings with the Choctaws, I have learned the interesting ways they get information from someone who is—shall I say reluctant?—to talk. Perhaps I will show you a few—for Danielle and Gaby?"

Sweat glistened on David's forehead in the gray light of dawn. "I know nothing about weapons, Beauvoir."

"Let me refresh your memory." The point of Rouen's knife cut into the flesh at the base of David's throat.

Sweat ran down the traitor's face. Blood oozed from the wound. Rouen increased the pressure, the blade sinking deeper into the flesh. His eyes round, David screamed.

"Tell me, David."

"The weapons come into the colony in crates of furniture I order from France."

"When is the next shipment?" Rouen eased the pressure on the knife slightly.

"In a week's time. A boat should arrive at Ship Island. My merchandise will be delivered by mule train."

"So that was what you were doing at Fort Louis—arranging your shipments. You cared nothing for Gaby. It was all a ruse." Rouen sat back on his haunches and toyed with his knife, his anger escalating at the callous way David had played with Gaby's life. "What do you plan to do with those weapons?"

David clamped his mouth shut, a stubborn look entering his eyes.

"You know you're a dead man. Will you die slowly and painfully or swiftly and with as little pain as possible?" Rouen asked in a lethal voice.

"More raids by the Chickasaws and some other tribes."

"Which ones?"

David's gaze darted about the cabin as if he sought an escape. Resigned to his fate, he looked back at Rouen. "The Natchez Indians. They hate the French as much as the Chickasaws. Possibly the Creek Indians. The English have approached them." David veiled his expression and lowered his gaze.

A feeling of foreboding twisted in Rouen's stomach. "What aren't you telling me?" He slashed David's linen shirt, exposing his chest, then traced a circle around each of the man's nipples, again drawing blood.

"They meet in two weeks' time to plan a raid on Fort Rosalie," David cried out, his gaze riveted to the blood trickling down his chest.

"Are any other Frenchmen helping you?"

"No."

Rouen stood, his expression set in a look of disdain. "I'm sure you feel better now that you have confessed your sins." He turned to his friend. "Claude, watch these two while I ride to the fort to inform the authorities."

Claude bowed deeply, sweeping his arm across his body. "My pleasure."

Seeing the feral gleam in his friend's eyes, Rouen

laughed and added, "Don't have too much fun with them."

"No more than the Indians did with Danielle's uncle."

Rouen left the cabin with David screaming for him to come back.

Danielle paced from one end of her bedchamber to the other. Her nerves were raw, taut with fatigue and worry. Where was Rouen? Why was he taking so long? She had prepared her speech hours ago. He hadn't trusted her.

She stopped by the tester. Maybe something went wrong and he was injured—or worse, dead. Her teeth dug into her bottom lip as she debated whether to go back to the cabin and see for herself. If everything was all right, Rouen wouldn't even know she had returned to check. If everything wasn't all right, she could save him—if she wasn't too late—and then tell him exactly what she thought of his high-handedness. She headed for the door.

It banged open. Rouen stood in the entrance like an avenging god. Danielle halted, swallowing several times when she saw the furious look on his face. She took a step back, her outrage forgotten in the wake of his.

"So you deign to let me know you are alive and everything is fine, *non?*" she said, taking the offense. She was the injured party in this whole affair, the one Rouen didn't trust enough to tell her about Armand David.

"*Madame,* everything is not fine." Lines of anger scored his features.

"You're alive. Armand is captured and will no longer hurt Gaby."

"True, but I must deal with a wife who disobeys her husband. Did I not specifically request that you *not* help Gaby? You almost got yourself and Gaby killed."

She took another step back.

"You believe, do you not, that a wife should respect her husband's wishes?"

Danielle clasped her hands in front of her, her fingers white from the strain.

"You believe, do you not, that a wife should trust her husband?"

She twisted her hands together, her gaze flitting away from his intense, brooding one.

"What have you to say?"

She met his look, her anger pushing to the foreground. "Why didn't you trust me enough to tell me Armand was a traitor? Why didn't you trust me enough to let me know your plans?" She lifted her chin to emphasize her own indignation.

"I was afraid you would say something to endanger yourself. I couldn't risk that. I see now I was wrong to stay silent."

Her enraged emotions deflated, leaving her feeling adrift, not quite sure what to do.

"Did you honestly think I would leave Gaby at David's mercy?"

She had been terribly wrong about Rouen. Hurt entered his eyes, and she hated being the cause of that. "The men I have known wouldn't have cared about Gaby or any woman. I acted. I didn't think."

Rouen was in front of her instantly, hauling her

up against him. "I am not the Marquis. I am not David. For that matter, I am not your Pierre."

"I know," she whispered. Her throat constricted. She had vowed she would never say words of love to him again. Pride held her silent.

"If this marriage is to work, we must trust each other, Danielle. I trust you. You will have to trust me."

"I know." She squeezed her eyes closed to keep the tears at bay.

"Look at me, *ma petite.*"

The sudden gentleness in his voice unleashed her emotions. As she opened her eyes, a tear fell on her cheek. "I know we had an arrangement, that love was not a part of it but—"

"Danielle, I love you." His fingers delved into her thick hair while his mouth crushed hers beneath his.

His declaration took her by surprise. She tried to comprehend his words, but she couldn't think straight while he was kissing her so passionately. She surrendered to his plundering tongue, to the caress of his hands, savoring his possession.

When he looked down at her, she finally realized her husband had said he loved her. "Rouen, are you sure?"

He chuckled. "Quite. It wasn't something I planned, but I am sure."

"Oh, what a relief." She sagged against him, laying her head near his heart, comforted by its strong, steady beat. "Now you won't mind that I love you. I thought that would complicate things, that you didn't want to hear that from me again."

He lifted her face and looked her in the eye. "You

can say it to me every day for the rest of our lives. I won't tire of it."

"I love you, Rouen."

"What shall we do about it?"

"Cement the alliance. I want children. Lots of children."

His smile warmed her insides, turning everything to liquid heat. He backed her up against the tester. "Isn't that interesting? We seem to want the very same thing. Shall we start right now?"

"I thought you would never ask." Danielle threw herself into his arms and kissed him long and hard.

FOURTEEN

One year later

"Be careful with that." Danielle hurried forward, ready to catch the hand-carved cradle that was being loaded in the wagon.

Rouen clasped her upper arms from behind and pulled her back against him. "Don't worry, *ma petite.* Everything that is important will get to France in one piece."

"It's just that Claude made that cradle for Alon. He spent months working on it. I want our other children to have it when they are born."

"And they will. I promise," he whispered against her ear right before nibbling on it.

She snuggled back more comfortably into his embrace. "*Monsieur,* we're in public."

"I can remedy that." He tugged her toward the house.

She laughed. "I must nurse Alon in a few minutes, finish Anne's new dress for this afternoon, then help Marte with the preparations for our farewell party. In a few hours we will have forty guests here, hungry and ready to celebrate."

"Excuses, excuses."

Turning within the circle of his arms, she leaned back to stare up at him. "I love you, Rouen Beauvoir."

His eyebrow rose. "What's going on in that pretty little head of yours?"

"You don't want to hear that I love you?"

"Every day. But I know you, Danielle. Something is going on."

She tilted her head to the side as though contemplating what to tell him. "I received two letters on the ship that arrived yesterday. One was from Sister Mary Catherine. She wrote to inform me that the Marquis was arrested for my mother's murder. It was quite a scandal. Do you know anything about that?"

He glanced toward the wagon. "I asked my father to look into the matter. I told you I would see that he paid for her death."

She knew it had taken a lot for Rouen to ask his father for anything. Love swelled in her chest. She stood on tiptoe and kissed him on the cheek. "Thank you, Rouen."

"Certainly, woman, you're more grateful than that."

She wound her arms around his neck and pulled his head down toward hers. She laid her mouth upon his, her tongue pushing inside to sample him. Right before she drew away, she nipped his lower lip.

"Who was the other letter from?" he asked, his eyes glinting with desire.

"Pierre."

Rouen stiffened.

"You have nothing to worry about concerning

Pierre. I don't love him. He is not the one I trust with my life. You are."

"Why did he write to you?"

Danielle heard the strain in his voice and smiled. "To ask my forgiveness and to let me know there were no gambling debts that his father owed the Marquis. He had lied to me about why he was marrying Margot. He didn't want me to come back to France and find out the truth from someone else."

"I should be glad he is a coward. Otherwise we wouldn't have met."

"He's paying for that cowardice now. He and Margot are outcasts at court. My stepsister is eating all the time and wants nothing to do with him."

"Then I won't have to call him out when we return to France."

A loud cry pierced the morning air. Danielle and Rouen looked toward the house.

"Our son is calling." Rouen placed his arm about her shoulder to escort her inside.

Gaby emerged from the house, holding Alon. "He definitely has his father's temper." She placed the baby in Danielle's arms. "Hopefully mine will be more like Claude, calm and even-tempered."

"Claude?" Danielle asked. Alon settled down and sought her breast.

Gaby sought her husband among the men by the wagon. "Yes, of course, Danielle." When her gaze found him, she lit up with a smile, patting her slightly rounded stomach.

When Alon couldn't find what he was looking for, his tiny face screwed into a frown and he let out a wail. Danielle wasted no more time getting inside and sitting down to feed her son. As he nursed,

Rouen came to stand next to her, staring down at Alon.

"Thank you, Danielle, for my son."

She glanced up at her husband. "You're welcome." When she saw him scan the house he had built out of the wilderness, piece by piece, she said, "I have come to appreciate the beauty of this place, but I am glad we are returning home. You do not mind leaving?"

"There will always be a part of me here. Claude and Gaby will carry on for us and maybe someday one of our children will return to the New World. But my place, *our* place, is in France. I have learned I can be my own man anywhere. Freedom is a state of mind." He leaned down and kissed her while his son continued to nurse, a sense of peace deep within him.

Hi, readers,

I've been writing and successfully selling for the past nineteen years. Making up stories with happy endings is a wonderful creative outlet. When I'm not writing, I'm teaching or reading books. I live with my husband, son, and two dogs. I grew up in Biloxi, where *Louisiana Bride* takes place almost three hundred years ago. I enjoyed trying to envision how the area would have been when it was first settled by the French. I would love to hear from you. You can write me at P. O. Boz 2074, Tulsa, OK 74101 or visit my Web page: http://members.aol.com/APR427.

Shauna Michaels